Logan searched ahead for an escape and spotted an alley on the left.

He quickly changed lanes. The car slid wildly on the wet pavement for a moment. He saw Skyler put her hand on the dash to brace herself for another impact. Wouldn't happen. Not if he had anything to say about it. He wouldn't let anything bad happen to her again.

"Hold on tighter," he warned. "We're turning left into an alley ahead."

"At this speed? In front of all this traffic?" Anxiety lifted her voice higher.

"I can do it. You could, too. We're both trained for this very thing, but Clyde isn't. He'll never make the turn." Logan squeezed her hand. "You trust me?"

"I trust you to keep me safe."

He heard the hesitation in her tone. Likely because she didn't trust him in any other area of life, not because she didn't believe he could handle this maneuver. Not something he could focus on now and safely evade the Jeep on their tail.

He let go of her hand and gripped the wheel. "Here we go."

Books by Susan Sleeman

Love Inspired Suspense

High-Stakes Inheritance
Behind the Badge
The Christmas Witness
*Double Exposure
*Dead Wrong
*No Way Out
*Thread of Suspicion
*Dark Tide
Holiday Defenders
    "Special Ops Christmas"
†*Silent Night Standoff*

*The Justice Agency
†First Responders

SUSAN SLEEMAN

grew up in a small Wisconsin town, where she spent her summers reading Nancy Drew and developing a love of mystery and suspense books. Today she channels this enthusiasm into hosting the popular internet website www.thesuspensezone.com and writing romantic suspense and mystery novels.

Much to her husband's chagrin, Susan loves to look at everyday situations and turn them into murder-and-mayhem scenarios for future novels. If you've met Susan, she has probably figured out a plausible way to kill you and get away with it.

Susan currently lives in Oregon, but has had the pleasure of living in nine states. Her husband is a church music director and they have two beautiful daughters, a very special son-in-law and an adorable grandson. To learn more about Susan, please visit www.susansleeman.com.

SILENT NIGHT STANDOFF

SUSAN SLEEMAN

HARLEQUIN® LOVE INSPIRED® SUSPENSE

Recycling programs
for this product may
not exist in your area.

LOVE INSPIRED BOOKS

ISBN-13: 978-0-373-44633-9

Silent Night Standoff

Copyright © 2014 by Susan Sleeman

www.Harlequin.com

Printed in U.S.A.

Peace I leave with you; my peace I give you.
I do not give to you as the world gives.
Do not let your hearts be troubled and do not be afraid.
—*John* 14:27

For my family who is always there for me.

ONE

The gun came out of nowhere.

A hard kick of adrenaline stole Skyler's breath. She raised her hands and backed away, the urge to reach for her own weapon nearly overpowering her good sense.

"Everyone on the floor now!" the bank robber screamed.

Skinny with spiked hair, his eyes were glassy, his body jittery. Fidgety. He was coming down from some drug. Not a good thing. Drugs and money were the top causes of violence, and he had both of them spurring him on. Making him unpredictable.

Add a loaded weapon and Skyler had a dangerous combination staring her down.

She needed to tread lightly. Forget about the gun in her purse for now. Do as he commanded.

She pulled in a few cleansing breaths and helped a pregnant woman settle on the cold tile floor of the Portland Community Bank, then took a seat with the other terrified customers.

She'd messed up. Big-time. Missed seeing the team dubbed by the media as a modern-day Bonnie and Clyde, but she hadn't been paying attention.

She wasn't on duty. She'd just stopped in to cash a check for her upcoming Christmas party for homeless families. A worthy cause, for sure, but she was a deputy sheriff and a hostage negotiator on the county's First Response Squad, for crying out loud. She was trained to read people, and she'd failed Cop 101.

Her training officer's voice rang in her head. Always know your surroundings. Always be alert and ready for anything. Serve and protect the innocent.

Protect, Skyler! How can you protect if you don't know what's going on?

Focus. Now. Before it's too late and someone gets hurt.

She watched Bonnie, a thin woman with dead eyes, calmly herd three customers from the teller windows to sit nearby. She shot across the room to retrieve the balding bank manager. That left three tellers standing behind the counter, all gaping at Clyde, his gun trained on them.

"My baby." The pregnant woman cradled her swollen belly as her terrified gaze flitted around the space. "I've got to get out of here."

"It's okay," Skyler whispered. "You and your baby will be fine. Just fine."

"You don't know that." Panic took her voice high.

Hoping to redirect the woman's thoughts before one of the robbers singled them out, Skyler asked, "What's your name?"

"Faith."

"Well, Faith, I do know we all have a much better chance of avoiding injury if we keep calm and do everything we're told."

"No talking!" Clyde spun on them and locked gazes with Skyler.

For the first time since they'd drawn their weapons, Skyler doubted her abilities. Doubted she'd be able to end this situation without anyone getting hurt. Not without her team. On duty, she'd have a sniper at the ready. Medical support waiting. A trained supervisor calling the shots as he did for all crisis situations in the county.

"I've got to get out of here." Faith struggled to stand. Skyler stilled her as Bonnie shot across the room toward them.

Bonnie bent low, her scraggly blond hair falling over her face. She jabbed her gun at Faith's chest. "Are you deaf, lady? He said no talking."

"Easy," Skyler said, the word slipping out before she thought better of it.

Bonnie pawed her hair from her eyes and glared in reply. Skyler should be afraid, but her anger fired hotter, blotting out her fear. Faith didn't deserve to be frightened like this. The terror would live with her—with everyone in the room—for the rest of their lives.

Skyler needed to do everything she could to minimize their trauma. That meant holding her anger in check so she was ready to act if she could do so safely.

"Man the door, Bonnie," Clyde said, his focus returning to the tellers.

Bonnie kept narrowed eyes fixed on Faith until she reached the door and turned her back.

Perfect. Just the distraction Skyler needed.

She shifted her body for privacy, opened the message screen on her phone and typed, 211 bank 23rd & Glisan. Bonnie and Clyde. 2 Glock 9mm. She sent the message to squad leader, Jake Marsh, then dialed his number and lowered her in-call volume to zero to keep the robbers from hearing Jake answer.

When she saw that the call had connected and knew he was on the line, she switched to speaker so he could listen in. She palmed her phone—microphone facing out—and turned back to wait for her team to arrive.

"Put all of your cash in the bag." Clyde unfolded a worn duffel bag and tossed it onto the counter in front of the first teller.

"Move it along, Clyde," Bonnie yelled from her post at

the front door. "All we need is for a customer to show up and call the cops."

Clyde slid over to the next teller. "Your turn. Make it quick."

Skyler sat quietly, praying her squad arrived soon to set up their command center and get everyone out before the situation turned ugly.

Time ticked by.

Slowly. Painfully. A minute feeling like an hour.

The soothing strains of "Silent Night" played from the speakers, but nothing was calm or bright in this room. Just the opposite.

Skyler was aware of every breath she took. Of the perspiration sliding down her back. Of her purse lying against her leg, the gun inside. The change in Faith's breathing and the face of an elderly man wearing a tattered suit reddening like a ripe tomato.

Why did they have to have a heat wave in December of all times? The seventy-plus afternoon temps made it seem more like an Oregon summer. Mix that with the fear pulsing around them and the space felt like a muggy, breath-stealing jungle. A situation that could cause panic.

"People are hot and looking like they might pass out," Skyler said to Clyde. "Would it be okay if they took off their coats or sweaters?"

"Not happening." He didn't even bother to look at the group.

"I'm really worried about them." Skyler grabbed a brochure from a rack and fanned Faith. "Especially Faith here. Her pregnancy makes her much hotter than the rest of us."

Bonnie spun. "Another word out of you, and I'm coming over there to shut you up," she shouted, her face tightening in anger.

Skyler could see Bonnie was starting to lose it, so Skyler clamped her mouth shut while continuing to fan Faith. When a police siren sounded nearby, Skyler held her breath, fearing that her worst nightmare was coming true. It was protocol not to run the siren and take cover out of view when responding to a robbery. The procedure kept robbers from panicking and causing a deadly hostage situation.

Please let it be a simple traffic stop. Not a rookie flying high with adrenaline and failing to follow procedures.

The *whoop, whoop, whoop* of the siren wound closer, an eerie warning of problems to come. The wail stopped just outside.

No. The officer *was* responding to the robbery.

"Cops!" Panic flooded Bonnie's face as she ran across the room and tugged on Clyde's arm. "We need to get out of here now."

Clyde jerked his arm free and jumped onto the counter. He shoved the gun into the nearest teller's forehead. Without a siren, Bonnie and Clyde would've left the bank, giving waiting officers the chance to arrest them. Now, combine their panic with drugs that were known to cause paranoid psychosis, and Skyler faced a full-blown crisis.

Clyde got in the teller's face. "You press the panic button?"

"No." Her terrified voice cut to Skyler's core.

"Then who did?" He stepped along the counter, his sloppy tennis shoes slapping on the Formica as he pointed his gun at the male teller. "You?"

He shook his head, his eyes cutting around the space as if searching for a way out.

"How about you?" Clyde waved his gun at the last teller. "N-no."

"One of you had to or the cops wouldn't be here this fast. I'm going to start shooting you one by one until you tell me who sounded the alarm."

"No, Clyde," Bonnie begged. "Let's get out of here while we can."

"The cops have to get organized, and this won't take long." Clyde lowered his finger to the trigger guard and sneered down at the tellers. "Who's first?"

The female tellers started sobbing. The male's face paled. Skyler couldn't let them pay for her actions.

"Stop!" She came to her feet.

Clyde whipped around. He pointed his weapon at Skyler's heart, but she didn't back away.

"It was me. I texted a cop friend of mine," she said, purposely not mentioning she, too, was a deputy. She held her breath as she waited for him to fire.

He jumped from the counter and marched across the room. She was hyperaware of every second passing while he advanced on her. His baggy jeans whispering. The *thump, thump, thump* of his shoes. His body odor and foul breath.

Inches away, he pressed the gun into her mouth and held out his hand. "Give me your phone."

She resisted gagging on the cold steel and handed over her phone. The acrid smell of burned carbon filled her nostrils. He'd fired this gun before. Maybe it was the same gun used to kill two hostages in California.

Please, God, don't let his finger slip.

He turned his attention to the phone and woke up the screen. She knew once he discovered her ongoing call to Jake, he'd squeeze the trigger, ending her life. In all her negotiations, she'd never been this close to death. Sweat rolled down her back and beaded above her lip.

"Clyde, c'mon," Bonnie said. "We stay here any longer and the place will be swarming with cops."

Yes, Clyde, run. Now. Fast. Down the street and into the arms of my team.

He stared at Skyler's phone and didn't respond.

Please, God, don't let this be the end.

A sick smile spread across Clyde's thin lips, revealing teeth rotted from a meth addiction and confirming her suspicions of drug use. She braced herself for his finger curling on the metal. The report of gunfire. The weapon jerking in her mouth. Death taking hold.

"Jake, huh," he said, his sneer widening. "You didn't just text him—you called him, too." He lifted the phone to his mouth. "Well, *Jake*." He jiggled the gun, and Skyler's heart threatened to stop beating. "Sorry you hurried on over here. You cost this pretty little lady her life."

His finger slid to the trigger. "Say buh-bye to Jake, missy. It's the last thing you'll ever do."

Adrenaline spurring him on, FBI Agent Logan Hunter approached the police barricade outside the bank robbery in progress. He'd caught the perfect break. He'd just gotten into town, when the call came in about Bonnie and Clyde. His team was en route to the standoff, but as the case agent tasked with bringing in the robbers, Logan was in the right place at a critical moment. True, he still had to convince the local authorities to let him in on the action, but that was a piece of cake.

He paused to take in the scene and plan his approach. He'd been briefed on the unique First Response Squad— a division of the county sheriff's department—on the way over. He spotted the man who was clearly their commander, Lieutenant Jake Marsh, standing outside their large white command truck. He was talking to the team's sniper, who was unzipping a rifle case. Both were dressed in the team uniform of black tactical pants and polo shirts, but the sniper added a tactical vest and loaded it with extra ammo.

Marsh, feet planted wide, stood calmly, his focus intense. The sniper was jumpy, his foot tapping on the concrete. As Logan climbed over the barricade, the sniper took off across the street to get into position for a kill shot should it become necessary. Marsh stepped to another team member settling a small orange case on a small robot. Likely a negotiator—

an *additional* negotiator, since Logan had heard that another one was already in the building. The man didn't rush, but moved with purpose and double-checked each step. Obviously not his first hostage standoff.

The case held a phone connected by a long cable to the command truck and would provide direct communications to the robbers. *If* the team could get them to take the phone. That was a big if as they wouldn't need a throw phone if the robbers had answered the bank phone or kept in touch on the inside negotiator's cell.

As Logan approached, he searched for the bomb expert and the EMT who rounded out the team of six. He found neither and assumed they were in the truck. He headed straight for Marsh.

Marsh looked up, his eyes narrowing.

Logan flashed his badge. "I hear you have a team member inside."

Marsh's brows shot toward his thick black hair. "This is your concern, why?"

"Bank robbery." Logan knew his response was lame, but the bureau's jurisdiction over bank robberies was his only way into the action. He hoped Marsh played nice and let him participate in the negotiations.

"The investigation is all yours." Marsh made strong eye contact. "*After* my team resolves the standoff. Until then, you stand down."

The lieutenant's rebuff should have angered Logan. Instead, he respected the guy for standing up to an agent. But Logan had no intention of sitting back. Of letting the locals do their thing when his future promotion at the FBI depended on him arresting Bonnie and Clyde. A promotion that should win him the first hint of respect in his demanding father's eyes.

"I'm not asking to take charge of the standoff," Logan said. "But our agency has been tailing this pair for months now. My information could be invaluable in your efforts here."

"Fine," Marsh said. "Speak only when asked and you can stay."

Right. Real team player.

Schooling himself not to get mad, Logan followed Marsh to the mobile command center. The negotiator climbed the stairs after Marsh and Logan trailed them onboard the state-of-the-art truck.

"Everybody," March called out as he stepped to a communications suite holding three monitors, "the suit is Special Agent Hunter. He's heading up the bureau's investigation into Bonnie and Clyde."

Marsh snapped on a headset, then clamped a hand on the shoulder of a scrawny young man who sat behind a computer watching a live feed of the bank's exterior from the truck's rooftop camera.

"Where're we at, Darryl?" Marsh asked.

Darryl didn't look up from his keyboard. "Should be tapped into the bank security feed in a few seconds."

As Marsh stared over Darryl's shoulder, Logan quickly assessed the team. The negotiator had stopped next to a control station for deploying robots, where a muscle-bound guy sat tapping his foot. The bombs guy, Logan suspected. A woman he assumed was the EMT checked supplies in the medical bay that formed the back of the truck. Everyone was somber and intense.

"Okay, people." Marsh turned to the group as he glanced at his watch. "We're hitting the ten-minute mark since the call came in. Every second brings us closer to the outcome we're hoping to avoid. Based on the robbers' prior behavior, there's a good chance of casualties here. Brady's in place and ready to take the shot if necessary."

The sense of fear for their team member in the hands of

two unpredictable and armed robbers hung in the air, and the mood darkened even more.

"We're in," Darryl announced, drawing everyone's attention. "Let me dial in on the action." He clicked a few keys. Suddenly the screens lit with live footage from the bank's interior.

Logan focused on the monitor. Clyde flashed onto the screen, holding the negotiator at gunpoint. Logan's mouth went dry, and his pulse skipped a beat.

"Skyler? The negotiator inside is Skyler Brennan?" His strangled cry brought all eyes toward him.

"You know Skyler?"

Know her? He'd dated her for a year and had nearly let himself forget his goals and fall in love with her.

"You're her suit?" the EMT asked. "The one who dumped her?"

Logan didn't know how to answer, so he said nothing.

"Darcie?" Marsh asked.

"He dated Skyler before she joined the squad. Chose his career over her and moved away for the job. Guess he's back now." Darcie's acerbic tone conveyed what she thought of him.

She kept watching him, so he turned his attention back to the screen. As he focused on Skyler's brave face, his pulse beat triple time. She looked the same. Short, curvy with red hair. She had a sweet girl-next-door face devoid of any makeup. Her hair was currently secured in two small pigtails that gave her a pixie look.

Vulnerable. The word shot into his brain as a chill iced him over. She'd been training for a position like this when he'd met her, but as a woman in a largely male field, and with only three years as a detective under her belt, he never really thought she'd get the job. Or maybe the real issue was he'd avoided thinking about the danger a negotiator's job involved to keep his fears at bay.

She didn't act afraid. She appeared calm and in control, her attention fixed on Clyde, who had his gun sighted on her.

It seemed as if the room collectively drew in, then held a breath, waiting for their sniper to take Clyde out. No response. No crack of a rifle disturbing the peace.

"Can't you people do something?" Logan asked, surprised that his voice was as panicked as a scared little girl. "Clyde's not averse to killing."

Marsh eyed him. "Skyler knows to give us a signal if she's in danger."

Or not. "She's not a negotiator now. She's a hostage just like the others. She might have sound training, but the stress she's under means she's not 100 percent in there."

"I've got it covered," Marsh said calmly. "If I think lives are in danger, I won't wait for Skyler's signal. I'll give the go-ahead for Brady to fire."

Logan appreciated Marsh's calm approach and his willingness to step in if Skyler faltered, but it did nothing to relieve Logan's helpless feeling. He wanted to control the team. Make them act when seeing one of their own in danger didn't seem to faze them.

The atmosphere was tense, the space closing in on him, the air disappearing, and they just stood. Calmly. Watching it happen. A necessary trait for a squad called to respond to all sorts of emergencies, but Logan wouldn't—couldn't—do the same thing.

Not now. Not when Skyler's life was on the line.

TWO

Skyler ignored Clyde's bruising grip on her arm as he dragged her across the space and out of view of the others. He released her arm, and she sagged to the floor.

"Are you sure about this?" Bonnie yelled from the other side of the room where she continued to guard hostages.

"Positive." Clyde glared at Skyler. "We're better off with her alive. For now, anyway. She's friends with the cops. We can use her connections to get out of here." He grabbed her purse and started pawing through it.

Praising God for the reprieve, Skyler gulped in deep breaths, but the sun's warm rays beating through the window ratcheted up the tension already sizzling through the room, making it hard to breathe. To think. To act. For her and the robbers. Especially Bonnie. She was losing it, barking orders at the other hostages, her voice high and shrill. With every second that passed, she behaved more erratically and was clearly heading for a meltdown.

"Oh, yeah! Better than I thought." Clyde pulled his hand out and held up her deputy's shield and gun for Bonnie to see. "She's one of them. Her name's Skyler Brennan. Deputee Skyler Brennan."

Bonnie shot across the room, her gaze darting about, her expression that of a trapped animal. She stopped next to Clyde where they could keep an eye on Skyler and the other hostages at the same time.

"I don't like this, Marty," Bonnie whispered loudly enough for Skyler to hear.

Marty? His name's Marty?

"Relax, Nicole," Marty whispered back, though he danced on the balls of the feet, proving he wasn't the least bit relaxed himself.

Good. They didn't think Skyler could hear them. Now she knew both of their names. Not that she'd use them now. It would spook them more. But if they somehow managed to evade capture and Skyler got out of there alive, detectives would have a solid lead to go on.

"Brennan's our ticket out of here," Marty continued, louder now. "They'll never try to hurt us with her as our hostage."

Ha! Shows what they know. If Skyler gave FRS sniper Brady Owens the signal, he would fire. Didn't matter if she was threatened. Didn't matter if she might die in the process. He was trained to shoot the moment she tugged on her earlobe. Jake was the only person who could override the signal.

"So let's get on with it, then." Nicole turned to go back to her post.

Skyler couldn't let Nicole walk away and miss this opportunity to encourage their surrender. "There's another solution," Skyler offered calmly.

Nicole snorted. "Like we'd listen to you."

Skyler infused her tone with sincerity. "Despite what you think, I care about your safety and don't want to see you get hurt."

"We won't," Nicole fired back. "Not with you as our shield."

"See, there's where you're wrong. I can't protect both of you from all sides. You've always gotta worry about a bullet from some rogue cop trying to make a name for himself by bringing in Bonnie and Clyde. Or even a panicked rookie. Surrendering right now is the only way to guarantee you won't get hurt."

Nicole clapped her hands over her ears. "Shut up. Just shut up already." She scrunched her eyes closed for a long moment, then opened them and lowered her hands. "C'mon, Clyde. We gotta move before the cops get better organized."

"Start Brennan heading to the back door. I'll get the bag." He jogged to the counter.

Nicole raised her weapon and stepped forward. "Over there, Brennan. Next to preggers."

Skyler didn't think Nicole really planned to shoot her, but as time passed, she'd become shaky and sweaty. Likely her drugs were wearing off. With the bank surrounded by law enforcement, she was desperate. Unstable. Skyler had best do as asked.

"It's not too late to surrender," Skyler suggested as she started to rise. "I'll make sure you get a fair hearing."

"Ha!" Nicole's eyes flashed in anger. "I'm not going to jail. Not when we have you. We'll head out the back just like L.A."

Skyler remembered hearing about L.A., where the hostages were killed in a shoot-out with the police. "That didn't end so well."

"We came out just fine. Didn't we, Bonnie?" Marty winked at Nicole.

She nodded. "And we will again. It's better than waiting here for your buddies to storm the bank."

"Okay." Marty hefted the bag onto his shoulder. "Let's do it."

Skyler needed to try one more time to stop them. "Don't do this. Listen to me. If you surrender now, I can guarantee you won't be shot, but in the alley I—"

"Shut up!" Nicole screamed, her eyes wide as she charged at Skyler. "We know what we're doing. I've had about enough of your double-talk. We don't need your help. Just." She raised her gun and poked the barrel into Skyler's forehead, and she could almost smell Nicole's desperation. "Shut." She moved closer. "Up."

She'd lost control. Skyler shot a quick look at Marty, hoping for his help in calming Nicole.

A gunshot split the quiet. The window shattered. Glass exploded through the air.

The gun jerked from Skyler's head. She turned her gaze back to Nicole, but heard a loud thump even before she saw Nicole lying on the floor, a fatal gunshot wound to her head. *Brady.*

"No!" Marty screamed. "Nicole!" He dropped the bag and raced to Nicole. He checked her pulse though there was no way she could've survived.

Jake must've thought Nicole planned to kill her and given Brady the order to take the shot. It was an order he rarely gave, and one that haunted him every time.

"This is your fault." Marty glared at Skyler. "You did this. You killed her. If you hadn't made that call…" His eyes were wild now. Crazy and panicked. Breathing hard, his gaze darted around the space. He jumped to his feet, grabbed Skyler's hair and dragged them both out of sniper range.

At the teller window, he released her and snatched her phone from the counter. "Let's see what your buddy Jake thinks about this."

As he fumbled with her phone, Skyler checked on the hostages. Red and perspiring, Faith fanned her face. The others seemed too stunned to move. At least they were spared seeing Nicole's body.

"Big mistake. Big, big mistake," Marty yelled into the

phone. "You have three minutes to clear the alley of cops. You got it? Or I start killing the hostages one by one."

Sharp gasps and sobs came from the group.

"C'mon, Marty—talk to me," Jake said calmly over the phone's speaker. "We can work this out."

"It's too late for working anything out. In three—no, make that *two* minutes and forty-five seconds—I'm heading out the back door with your girl, Brennan. I want all barricades removed. If I see an officer or even smell one of you anywhere near the alley, she will die instantly. You got that? Instantly." He hung up before Jake could pass the phone to Archer to begin negotiations as protocol dictated.

Marty looked at Faith. "Get the bag."

"I c-can't. Please. My baby."

"Now!" he screamed.

"You can do it, Faith," Skyler encouraged.

Sobbing, Faith struggled to her feet and picked up the bag. Skyler wanted to offer to take it, but Marty had clearly reached the end of his rope. Any word from her might set him off. If they were in sniper range and she was in a position to signal Brady, she'd be tugging her ear, but Marty knew to stay back. He took the bag from Faith and harnessed it across his chest.

"You first," he said to Faith. "Get in front of me."

Faith complied, and Marty stepped behind Skyler. He shoved her toward Faith, but Skyler held her ground. If Marty got them outside, she feared they could be killed just like the hostages in the L.A. standoff.

"Fine, stand there." He jabbed the gun in the back of her head. "It's no skin off my nose. I have plenty of other hostages to choose from. I'm more than happy to make you pay for Nicole's death right here, right now. Or you can make yourself useful and buy a few hours before I pull the trigger. Your choice, but either way, Dep-u-tee, you're going to die today."

* * *

In the alley behind the bank, Logan could still hear the crack of the gunshot. Feel his stomach cramping as the blast reverberated through the air. He wanted to charge toward the threat to see if Skyler was okay. Instead, he'd moved into the shadows in case Bonnie or Clyde came out the back door as they'd done in L.A.

Clearly, the officers stationed at the mouth of the alley didn't possess this bit of intel. If they did, they'd insist on joining Logan. He wouldn't volunteer it, either. Not when one of them might be the rookie who'd escalated the stand-off. Logan couldn't risk Skyler's life. He was better off handling the takedown alone. If the robbers exited with Skyler or another hostage, Logan could save the hostage and arrest Bonnie and Clyde, thus securing his promotion. A win-win for everyone.

The cops suddenly sprang into action, putting Logan on full alert. They shot a quick look down the alley then disappeared from view. It was odd that they'd taken off, but maybe the gunshot meant the standoff was over. Or they were moving to a more strategic location. Logan wasn't going anywhere until he was certain Bonnie and Clyde weren't walking out this door.

He waited, gun at the ready, listening for any sound. With the usual traffic for this area cordoned off, it was eerily quiet. Time slowed to a trickle, the only sound the beat of Logan's heart thrumming in his ears. As he was ready to step out and reevaluate, a wailing alarm sounded from the back door's emergency exit bar.

He expected legions of cops to race down the alley, but the only movement he saw was the door slowly swinging open. A pregnant woman stepped out, a hairy arm snug around her neck, a handgun to her head.

Clyde? Had the sniper missed? What happened to Skyler?
Holding his breath, Logan sighted his weapon.

Hunched over, his head buried behind the pregnant woman for protection, Clyde exited next. A woman's arms were wrapped around his waist from the back.

Bonnie?

The trio continued in an awkward dance until Logan could finally identify Skyler as the woman in the rear. *Where is Bonnie?* Would she be following them in a moment, flanked by other hostages, or had she been taken out by the sniper?

Near the middle of the alley, the pregnant woman wobbled before dropping to her knees, keeling over in a faint. Clyde immediately pulled Skyler in front of him and put his back to the wall.

Logan needed to unsettle him again before he could lift his gun against Skyler. "FBI! Freeze!"

Clyde spun, dropped his arm from Skyler's waist and aimed his weapon at Logan.

"Drop it or I'll shoot!" Logan shouted.

"Logan?" Skyler cried out in surprise.

Clyde cocked his weapon. Logan fired. Skyler karate-chopped Marty's arm. His gun flew from his hand and skittered across the asphalt. His gasp of pain hunched him over, but he recovered quickly and grabbed Skyler's arm. He pulled her to his chest, using her as a shield and blocking Logan from getting off another shot. As Logan started closing in on his position, Clyde clearly knew his time was running out.

"Don't think this is over, Brennan," he screamed at her. "You will pay for Bonnie's death." He shoved her hard and took off.

Skyler's arms flailed out, trying to regain her balance, as Clyde ran toward the other end of the alley. Logan set off in pursuit, but came to a halt when Skyler slammed into a Dumpster and ricocheted off, plummeting to the ground.

Her head connected with a concrete barrier, and she landed by the pregnant woman.

"Skyler," he said, rushing to her side. She looked up at him for a long moment, her eyes going wide, then closing, and his heart refused to beat.

THREE

Blinding pain sliced through the back of Skyler's skull, blocking out all clear thought. She felt strong arms lift her from the ground and place her on a gurney. The movement increased her pain, and it was all she could do to hold back a cry of distress.

"Will she be okay?" Logan asked, his deep rumbling voice echoing down the alley.

Why is he here?

He'd left town two years ago after breaking up with her, and she hadn't seen him since. Maybe this was all a bad dream and she'd wake up soon. She still dreamed of him sometimes. Pleasant dreams of working on the shelter's Christmas party together. Something they'd done at this time of year. Would still be doing if he hadn't left her. Holding hands. Smiling. Then she'd wake up, remember and feel betrayed all over again.

She didn't want to talk to him, but she couldn't ignore him, either. She pried her eyes open and squinted into the sun. He came into view, standing tall above her. Dressed in a power suit, white shirt with gray tie, blue eyes ringed with black searching hers.

"Welcome back, sweetheart." His lips lifted in a sweet smile.

Her heart skipped a beat as she stared at him. At this man from her past. From her dreams.

"Look at me, Skyler," Darcie commanded from her other side.

Skyler turned her head, seeing her best friend's expression tight with concern. "Glad to see you're conscious again."

Skyler's head cleared and the afternoon's terrifying events came flooding back.

Clyde. The gun in her mouth. Its bitter taste. The stench of fear in the bank. Brady's shot. Leaving the building. Faith.

"Faith." Skyler tried to sit up. "How's Faith?"

"She's fine." Darcie gently pressed Skyler back down on the gurney. "On her way to the hospital just to be sure."

Skyler sighed. "Good. What about Clyde? Did he… Oh, Logan." She turned to look at him, surprised to find him still carefully watching her. "You were here. In the alley. Did Clyde…?"

"Get away?" He nodded. "Yeah. I got off one shot, but he's in the wind."

"There you are." Jake's angry voice came from the end of the gurney and suddenly Logan was jerked away. "What part of 'stay out of our way' didn't you understand, Suit? You could've gotten Skyler killed with that foolish stunt."

"Jake, wait," Skyler shouted, the effort making her head throb harder. "He saved my life."

"He could also have gotten you killed," Jake said. "And putting you in that situation wasn't his decision to make."

"But it worked out for the best, and he *did* save my life. Clyde blames me for Bonnie's death. If he'd kept me with him when he left, he would've killed me the minute he felt safe enough to do so."

"What?" Jake glanced at her over his shoulder but didn't release Logan.

"Clyde said if I hadn't texted you, they could've safely gotten out of the bank. So he blames me for Bonnie."

"That's what he meant," Logan muttered.

Jake glared at Logan. "Meant by what?"

"Before Clyde took off he said this wasn't over and Skyler would pay." Logan freed his jacket from Jake's grip and pressed out the wrinkle. "Besides the obvious threat here, it's also important to mention he called his partner Nicole. This is the first time we've heard her name, and he was under such duress we have to believe he wasn't making it up."

"His name is Marty," Skyler added.

"Marty?" Logan moved closer to her.

"Most of the time, they called each other Bonnie and Clyde, but in a private conversation when they didn't think I could hear, she called him Marty and he called her Nicole. He also screamed out her name when Brady took her out."

"And you're sure she called him Marty?"

"Positive."

Jake stepped to the gurney. "We're losing sight of the real issue here. Marty or Clyde or whatever you want to call him could be coming after Skyler."

Logan nodded. "That's a very real possibility."

Jake locked gazes with Skyler. "I don't want you going out on your own until this creep is brought in. Be on alert. In fact, you might want to stay home."

"Please." She rolled her eyes and even that slight movement brought pain. "If everyone on the squad took precautions like that each time someone threatened one of us, we'd all be hermits."

"Talk some sense into her, Darcie."

"She has a point. Tempers flare at these standoffs, but the suspect usually calms down." Darcie squeezed Skyler's hand. "Besides, I'm less worried about Clyde and more worried that she may need stitches and has a concussion." Darcie peered at her. "Loss of consciousness is a warning sign, honey. We should get you to the hospital."

"No." Skyler wished she could shake her head for emphasis without worsening her headache. "I'm fine."

Jake got in her face. "You lost consciousness. County procedure dictates a trip to the hospital to be checked out."

"Procedure, schmedure. I'm good to go." She tried to push him out of her way and sit up, but the arm Marty had grabbed buckled and a wave of dizziness assaulted her.

"You're fine?" Logan asked. "Explain why you can't sit up then."

She shot him a frustrated glare. "Okay. You all win. I'll get checked out, but I won't ride in the ambulance. My car's in the lot. I'll drive myself. It's less than a mile away. I'll be fine."

"Ha!" Jake said. "Like I'd let that happen with a head injury."

Darcie crossed her arms. "And if he did let you go, *I'd* stop you."

"I can give you a ride to the E.R.," Logan offered.

Skyler shot a look at him. He'd never voluntarily offer to leave his crime scene before inspecting it. Never put anything before work. Not even her. Next thing she knew pigs would fly overhead.

"I need to take your statement anyway," he went on. "We can do it on the way and save time."

Right, my statement. The job.

Skyler glared up at him, and tried to hide her disappointment, but she felt certain she hadn't managed it.

Nothing had changed. She still took second place with him. Third, if you counted his father, who truly came first since his career focus was aimed at making his father proud. That wouldn't change even if Logan was dating again. Making his father proud was Logan's top priority. Had always been his top priority, but Skyler had let the blush of love distract her and hadn't seen it. Until the day he'd walked out on her. That horrible, horrible day the week of Christmas, he'd proved he wouldn't be distracted from his mission to excel at the FBI.

Ever. Not even for a chance at love and a life with her.

Logan's phone chimed. Good. A distraction before Skyler's frustrated glare brought back memories he didn't want to think about. He'd suspected if he ever ran into her again, she'd be testy. But after two years, he didn't expect to see her eyes as cold as the day he'd told her he was taking the job at the FBI's Chicago office. Not one day since then had he found the weather in the Windy City to be colder than her expression that afternoon.

His fault. He shouldn't have gotten involved with her in the first place. Not when he was committed to reaching every milestone his FBI father had achieved, but doing so at a younger age. A relationship simply distracted him, and he couldn't afford to be distracted.

Especially not now. If he was successful in bringing in Bonnie and Clyde by Christmas, he'd become one of the youngest agents in the bureau's history ever promoted to assistant special agent in charge of a field office.

What father wouldn't be proud of that accomplishment?

Logan couldn't relax before then. Or even after. He'd still have to succeed at the job or risk losing the old man's approval. That meant undivided focus on the work.

He glanced at his phone. His team had arrived and it was time to move this along. He turned his attention back to Skyler.

"If you won't listen to my medical advice, Skyler," Darcie said, "there are plenty of shell-shocked witnesses inside who will." Though she sounded mad, Logan could see she really cared about Skyler before she marched off.

Logan waited for Marsh to follow, but he stood his

ground, as if he felt a need to protect Skyler. Logan got that. Seeing both Marsh's and Darcie's protectiveness, he could tell the team had formed a close bond. Something Logan had no time for, and yet, when he saw this kind of camaraderie, his solitary lifestyle seemed kind of lame.

Focus, man.

He turned to Skyler. "I hate to do this, but you were in physical contact with Marty and could have contact DNA on your clothes. We'll need to bag them before we leave."

"You can change into Darcie's extra scrubs in the rig," Jake offered.

"Fine." She looked at Logan as if she'd rather eat bugs than be this close to him. "It'll only take me a minute to change."

Logan ignored the way her coldness kept unsettling him and forced a cordial tone to his voice. "Take your time. My team has arrived, and I need to talk them for a minute, anyway. I'll send a tech out with an evidence bag for your clothes."

He headed for the lobby before he did something stupid like try to apologize to Skyler in front of Marsh. Not that Logan didn't owe her an apology. He did. He was still certain his decision to leave had been the right one, but he was genuinely sorry he'd hurt her in the process. For that, he'd apologize when the time was right.

Now he'd do his job and do it well.

He'd only seen the lobby on the truck's monitors, so he made a quick sweep of the place before stepping inside. Fellow agent Vince Wagner and the FBI's Evidence Recovery Team were already processing the scene, and a privacy screen had been erected to hide Nicole's body. The witnesses were no longer cowering on the floor by the counter but were sitting in chairs, chugging water.

Wagner glanced up, his eyes instantly narrowing as he stared at Logan. He'd gotten the same look from most of the

Portland agents. Logan understood their frustration. Totally understood it. They weren't pleased that the FBI had brought him in from another office to head up their investigation.

As far as they knew, he was there to use expertise gained on a similar robbery spree in Chicago, but it was more than that. Much more. His promotion was on the line. If he didn't succeed, he was on his way back to Chicago. So it was time to make nice with all the players and get this done.

He crossed the room to a forensic tech named Gary who looked like a thirtysomething version of Santa Claus.

Logan gave the guy instructions to gather Skyler's clothes, then asked for another bag to collect Faith's clothing at the hospital. "You'll also find a small amount of the suspect's blood in the alley to process. I'd like all the results rushed."

Gary snorted. "You and every other agent in the bureau. You'll need Inman's approval for a rush, and, even then, it'll likely take a week or so. Maybe more with the holidays."

He was right. The FBI lab had a backlog just like other law enforcement labs. Even with the special agent in charge of the Portland office requesting a rush, it was unlikely that the lab would move a bank robbery above homicides. It would take days for the results.

Logan held out a business card. "Mind giving me a heads-up if you find anything? I hate to wait for a report to circulate through channels when the other suspect is still on the loose."

"You got it." Gary pocketed the card in pants that hung below his belly. "I'll get those bags for you."

Logan turned to Wagner, who was watching him with tired eyes. He'd tipped his head, catching the overhead light on his bald scalp, and his lips were pursed below a graying mustache.

"Something bothering you?" Logan asked, hoping they could get any resentment out in the open and deal with it.

Wagner shook his head, but he still seemed uncomfortable with Logan's presence. For now, Logan would respect the guy's wishes not to talk about it. "I've completed a preliminary interview with Deputy Brennan and learned Bonnie and Clyde used the names Marty and Nicole when they thought no one else could hear them. I suspect those are their real names. Let's get this information to the rest of the team ASAP so they can get started on developing any additional leads."

"Finally, real names." Wagner sounded relieved. "Maybe people will stop calling them Bonnie and Clyde like they're some sort of heroes."

"I doubt the press will ever let it go. They thrive on the sensationalism the names garner," Logan said, then changed gears. "I'd like you to handle the scene while I transport Deputy Brennan to the hospital to check for a concussion. I'll finish my interview on the way." Logan didn't wait for Wagner's agreement but glanced at the privacy screen. "Is anyone from the medical examiner's office here yet?"

"No."

"When they arrive, make sure the body's printed and swabbed for DNA."

"And hope she has a record so we finally have a last name?"

"Exactly," Logan said, heading for the screen. "I'll take a quick look—then I'm out of here."

He stepped behind it and heard Wagner stop a few feet away. At the sight of the body, Logan swallowed hard. He didn't often deal with death in his job. He spent far more time pushing paper than anything, but Nicole wasn't the first shooting victim he'd seen. Sadly, she wouldn't be the last.

He squatted next to her. Not wanting to contaminate the evidence, he resisted touching her, but he did notice an odd distortion to her face.

"Check this out." He changed angles for a better view. "See the way her nose and chin have shifted?"

Wagner bent down. "Looks fake."

"Probably a prosthetic. Like you'd see in movie special effects. Maybe Marty or Nicole was a makeup artist. Would explain how they changed their appearance and why no one's been able to ID them."

"That would make sense since the first robbery took place in L.A."

"Make sure the ME takes great care when she removes the prosthetics so she doesn't damage them. Then get someone in the L.A. office to show them around Hollywood to see if anyone recognizes their work. And see if we can find out where the makeup supplies came from." Logan stood. "I'm sure I don't have to tell you to check with hospitals and clinics for a male of Marty's description with a gunshot wound."

Wagner nodded. "But honestly, the amount of blood you described in the alley suggests a superficial wound at most, and he won't likely need a doctor."

Logan decided not to lecture Wagner about following every lead no matter how small. It would only send a bad message that Logan micromanaged his team. That was the last thing he needed when he was trying to gain their cooperation. "Okay, I'm out of here. You have my cell, right?"

"Yes," Wagner said, appearing relieved Logan was leaving.

He headed for the door, stopping only to grab the evidence bag for Faith's clothing. He hated leaving the crime scene, but he believed Skyler was the key to cracking this ongoing investigation. As a trained officer, she'd likely noticed things during the robbery she didn't even know she'd seen. He would do his best to bring the memories to the surface before they had time to fade. Conducting the interview immediately was crucial.

He stepped outside and spotted Skyler sitting on the gurney, her face raised to the sun, the rich red highlights in her hair glinting in the warm rays. She'd replaced her frilly blouse with a faded scrub top, one pigtail stuck inside as if she'd dressed in a hurry. Despite a white bandage circling her head and baggy scrubs, she could still get his heart rate going.

As she lay on the gurney earlier, he'd noticed her wearing the same pair of jeans she'd loved when they were together. Except in the passing of time, she'd sewn colorful patches on them.

Just thinking about her free-spirited attire made him shake his head. The two of them were so different. He was a by-the-rules kind of guy, while she was easygoing, and yet they'd seemed almost perfect together.

Skyler suddenly looked at him. Her eyes communicated everything he knew she must be feeling—fear, anger, frustration.

A strong impulse to pull her into his arms, to shelter her from anything bad that might happen, had him taking a step back.

Don't go there, man.

She scooted to the edge of the gurney and planted a hand on her hip, a saucy expression on her face as her gaze settled on him. "You gonna stand there and stare at me or give me a ride?"

Right, like even if he wanted to hold her, she'd let him. She didn't accept help willingly. Outspoken and stubborn a good bit of the time, she stood on her own two feet. He hadn't forgotten that part of her personality. Not with the earful she'd given him when he'd decided to take the Chicago transfer. *That* he would never forget.

But he couldn't let it get in the way. Neither of them could. He needed her help to find the bank robber who would make Logan's career. And if his suspicions were correct, she needed him to keep her safe when Marty chose to attack.

FOUR

Logan took ground-eating strides toward Skyler. She should look away, but she couldn't take her eyes off him. He still infuriated her, but there was no denying he was something to look at—his chin wide and chiseled at hard angles, black hair thick and wavy. But it was those steely-blue eyes that had always gotten to her.

Intense. Dark. Maybe brooding at times.

So what? She couldn't stop the attraction, but she could stop herself from reacting to it and doing something stupid.

She fisted her hands, letting her nails bite into the sensitive flesh.

"Ready to go?" His mouth turned up in a lazy smile that was in direct contrast to his sharp focus, sending her pulse beating faster.

Disgusted with her betraying emotions, she pushed off the gurney faster than she should have and nearly lost her balance. She grabbed the wall to remain upright. She waited for the wooziness to pass, and caught sight of small dark stains dotting the alley. Marty's blood?

The feel and taste of his gun in her mouth came roaring back, and she swallowed hard, forcing down the ensuing panic. She wouldn't lose it now. Not here. Not in front of other law enforcement officers and certainly not in front of Logan.

"You actually hit Marty?" she asked, her voice a mixture of surprise and fear.

"Looks like I grazed him. My team is getting a bulletin out to local E.R.s and urgent care clinics in case he seeks medical attention." His phone rang, drawing his attention. He frowned at the screen, his deep scowl letting her know something was wrong.

"Excuse me a minute." He stepped out of earshot and paced. Back and forth. Over and over, quick steps across the alley and back, his hands plunged into his hair.

Seemed as if some things didn't change. He was still so driven to succeed he rarely stood still. It had taken her a year to get him to let his guard down and fully relax around her. He'd obviously returned to his breakneck pace in Chicago. She was sure he'd burn out long before he aged out of the bureau.

He stowed his phone, that frown deepening even more as he rejoined her. "We can go now."

She knew better than to ask about his call and marched toward the end of the alley. The hum of conversation from bystanders greeted her before she spotted them crowding behind wooden barriers. They pointed at her, and she heard cameras clicking. *Looky-loos.* She should've expected them, but she'd let her thoughts of Logan distract her. They were searching for anything sensational to grasp on to from the robbery. Maybe they'd tweet about it or post pictures on Facebook.

The last thing she needed today.

She slowly lowered her head and pushed forward to get out of the limelight as quickly as possible. Black wingtip shoes planted themselves in her path, forcing her to stop. She raised her head to find a male dressed in khakis, a white button-down shirt and a tie decorated with blindingly bright Christmas ornaments. He shoved a microphone into her face.

"Paul Parsons, News Channel Four. We heard that you were injured in the robbery, Deputy Brennan."

"I'm fine." Skyler tried to sidestep him, but he jumped in front of her.

"Are you working with the FBI to bring Clyde in?" Excitement lifted his tone.

Logan stepped forward. "Deputy Brennan's assisting us, as are all of the witnesses. Now if you'll excuse us, she needs to get to the E.R. to have her injury checked out." Logan shouldered the reporter out of Skyler's way and his hand came to rest on her back, urging her toward the crowd. This wasn't the time to argue against his touch, so she allowed it and hurried ahead.

"You heard it on our station first," Parsons said in his reporter's tone. "Portland's own Deputy Skyler Brennan will be working with the FBI on the Bonnie and Clyde investigation."

"Like that's newsworthy," Skyler mumbled and gingerly climbed over the barrier.

"Deputy Brennan, wait, please." Parsons's voice came from behind her.

Skyler groaned. Even if she could dredge up the energy to bolt away from him, she wouldn't. She couldn't afford to antagonize the press when she was still seeking positive publicity for the shelter's upcoming Christmas party. She turned slowly to keep the world from spinning.

Parsons rushed up to her again, the microphone now shoved in his pocket. "I'd really like to do an exclusive interview with you. People want feel-good stories this time of year, and we could combine your work for the shelter with the way you kept the hostages safe. You know, a local hero kind of thing."

She was far from a hero, but the shelter could use as much publicity as possible to raise awareness. Still, connecting the shelter to a violent bank robbery wouldn't be a good idea. "I really—"

"This isn't the time for this discussion," Logan barged in. "She needs to see a doctor." Before Parsons could respond, Logan parted the crowd with one hand and urged her forward with the other.

She allowed him to direct her, but her irritation flared with each step. How dare he presume to know what she wanted? Sure, she didn't want to do the interview, but he had no right to make choices for her. Not now. Not when he was out of her life.

After moving out of sight of the crowd, she shot him a testy look. "What was up with that? You have no right to speak for me. I let it go the first time Parsons asked because I didn't want to be interviewed today, but interfering the second time says you're planning to make a habit of it."

"What?" he asked, clearly confused.

"When we were together, it might've been different. I'd at least try to understand if you spoke up on my behalf like that, but you gave up that right when you walked out." She rushed ahead of him. The world whirled in front of her, and she instantly regretted it.

"Skyler, wait." He hurried up beside her and steadied her. She could barely abide his touch, but it was either his hand or a face-plant on the concrete.

"I'm sorry," he said sincerely. "I wasn't trying to talk for you—I just didn't like the way he kept stopping you from getting to the hospital."

She twisted to stare up at him, sending a breath-stealing jolt through her head. Or was it his nearness after all these years that took her breath away? Seeing his eyes up close. Smelling his expensive cologne. Remembering their time together, always remembering.

He didn't pull away or say a word. His gaze locked on hers.

"Skyler," he finally whispered as his hand lifted to her face. He brushed his fingers lightly over her cheekbone, his touch feeling like a branding iron. "I'm sorry for everything I put you through. I never wanted to hurt you."

Her heart leaped at the open regret in his voice, but his comment also reminded her of the lonely nights she'd spent at home after the Christmas holidays, longing to see him. She shook off his fingers and forced herself to move back. "As you said, now's not the time for such things. I really need to see that doctor."

He frowned and gestured down the street. "My car's at the end of the block."

His car. Here in Portland. Not in Chicago.

"When were you going to tell me you were back in town?" she blurted out before she thought better of continuing their personal discussion. "Or weren't you planning to contact me?"

"I haven't moved back here, Skyler."

Disappointment she didn't want to feel lodged in her throat, and she swallowed hard. "Then why are you working the bank robbery?"

"I was successful in solving a similar robbery spree in Chicago, so the bureau assigned me to head up this investigation."

Something in his tone led her to believe he wasn't being completely forthright with her. Not a surprise. He'd kept the job opportunity in Chicago from her for a month before telling her he was leaving, and he had even less reason to be candid now. But it still hurt. Would continue to hurt. Which was why she needed to give her statement and be done with this investigation.

He clicked the remote and unlocked his rental car. She jerked open her car door before he could get it for her as he'd frequently done in the past. She'd always considered him the perfect gentleman. He may still be a gentleman, but she now knew he was far from perfect.

She slid onto the buttery soft leather seat as he settled behind the wheel. He soon merged the car onto Twenty-third Avenue, but she didn't even notice the bustling traffic for the tension filling the car.

Thankfully, the hospital was nearby.

At a red light, he turned the knob on a portable police scanner. *Right.* His emotions weren't tainting the air. Only hers. He didn't feel the same distress. As usual, he was thinking about the job.

Good. His choice served as a reminder to be far more careful with her emotions around him.

He twisted his head around to check for cars, then switched lanes. "I'd forgotten about the crazy traffic in this neighborhood."

Small talk. Had they really come to this? "I'm sure Chicago has a trendy area with shops and restaurants like this," she replied.

"I don't get out much, so I couldn't say."

Not surprising. He probably ate all his meals at work or his apartment. It took time to make friends. To do things with them. Precious time he'd devote to getting ahead at the FBI.

How had she ever thought the two of them made a good couple? That she and anyone made a good couple? Her parents, with all their bickering and unhappiness, proved that marriage wasn't a good idea. With them as role models, how could she even think about finding lasting happiness in a relationship?

She stifled a sigh and stared out the window.

He glanced at her. "Tell me about the robbery."

Thankful to have a safe topic, she recounted the details. "I have a feeling Bonnie and Clyde are both into drugs.

Marty's teeth screamed meth user. Both their eyes were glazed, and they seemed to be coming down off something."

"The autopsy will confirm that." He clicked on a blinker. "Did you notice anything odd about their physical appearance?"

"Odd?" She thought for a minute, wincing when visions of Marty's angry eyes glaring at her over the gun barrel came roaring back. She took a deep breath and forced herself to replay the entire incident. "I remember thinking Nicole had a perfect complexion, which is odd for a drug user."

"Makeup."

"Excuse me?"

"She was wearing a prosthetic nose and heavy makeup to throw us off."

"Really?" Skyler swiveled to look at him. "How interesting."

"I'm guessing Marty wore theatrical makeup, too. But you didn't notice it up close?"

"No."

"What *did* you see?"

"Nothing. At least nothing else that I remember."

"You must've noticed something."

"Don't be so sure. All cops like to think we'll be cool and calm under pressure, but when your life is on the line..." She shrugged.

"Maybe it would help if you closed your eyes to visualize the scene."

She never wanted to close her eyes again. Never wanted to replay the memories of Marty and relive that fear. But if doing so aided in bringing Marty to justice, she'd try it.

She rested her head on the seat back and forced her eyes to close. Her other senses shot to life. She felt the cool air-conditioning blowing over her face. Smelled Logan's sandalwood cologne mingling with the car's pine air freshener.

Heard the bustling traffic. But her mind refused to go back to the bank.

Calm down, she told herself and pressed her fists against her knees.

Logan settled his hand over hers.

She jerked it free, her eyes flashing open.

"Relax," he said. "You're safe here."

Ha! She wasn't safe. At least not emotionally. Her reaction had nothing to do with the robbery and everything to do with him.

"Close your eyes again," he continued soothingly. "Concentrate on Marty. His clothes. His smell. His accent."

She closed her eyes but kept her hands out of Logan's reach. She dredged up Marty's voice as he talked to Nicole. "He didn't have an accent. Not even regional." Thinking about his smell, she flashed forward to the end when he'd forced her to put her arms around him. "He smelled like powder. Not baby powder, but like face powder. Maybe from the makeup."

"What about his body? Did he have a tattoo or other identifying marks?"

"Not that I remember. Plus, if he was going through all the trouble of changing his appearance, I doubt he'd let something like that show." She ran through the whole event, pausing at his latex gloves. "A ring. He wore a ring. It was large. Gold, no stone, but a raised top that had a symbol or words." She mentally zoomed in on it. "He wore latex gloves, so I couldn't make out the letters. Maybe it was a class ring."

"From a college?" Logan asked.

"He didn't seem like the collegiate type." She looked at Logan. "I'd put him in his early thirties, so it's doubtful he was still wearing a high school ring. College is a better guess, I suppose."

"We'll try to enhance the video to see if we can identify it, but if not, would you be willing to look at pictures of college class rings?"

"Sure, but without knowing anything about Marty or Nicole, how would you even know which colleges to begin looking at?"

"Though they've been quite successful, Marty and Nicole are amateur robbers, and amateurs often target banks close to home. Dumb, I know, but they do. So I'll go back to their first robbery and pull colleges in the general area."

"Maybe he'd recently moved there or he went to school out of state."

"You could be right, but despite their amateur status we have very little to go on, so this is as good of a place as any to start."

"You keep saying amateur, but their intrusion style behavior didn't fit an amateur's profile. Amateurs usually pass notes and don't carry weapons, right?"

His eyes widened in surprise, likely over her knowledge of bank robbers. "That's how they operated at first. But after the success of their first two holdups, they started showing up with guns."

The mention of guns sent Skyler flashing back to the moment Nicole lost her life, falling to the ground with a sickening thud. "We're only talking about Marty now."

"Right. Just Marty." Logan's fingers tightened on the wheel, going white from the tight grip. He came to a stop at a red light and met her gaze. "There may only be one of them now, but don't think that means you can let your guard down. Marty's the one who pulled the trigger on the hostages in L.A. and now he has a grudge to settle with you. That not only makes him dangerous, but deadly, as well."

For about the hundredth time, Logan paced past the large Christmas spruce scenting the E.R. lobby with fresh pine. It was amazing he even noticed the tree at all. Celebrating Christmas was the furthest thing from his mind right now. And he wasn't even thinking about the job. Concern for Skyler kept his thoughts occupied. She'd been with the doctors for three hours.

Maybe something was seriously wrong with her. Maybe he should march up to the desk to demand an update from the nurse.

He hadn't caught even a glimpse of Skyler since she'd rushed out of his car at the entrance, saying she'd find her own ride home. Of course, he didn't listen to her. He couldn't leave her alone here. So he'd parked and gone inside. After he'd collected Faith's clothing, he'd started passing the time by making phone calls, starting with Wagner.

Not that it moved the investigation forward. Wagner didn't find matching prints for Nicole in any of the databases. So she didn't have a record.

Strike one.

Logan called SAC Frank Inman to fast-track Nicole's lab work in the event she'd been a crime victim and her DNA was in a database. He'd agreed, but they both knew it was an extreme long shot.

Strike two.

Calls finished and still no Skyler, he tried to make a to-do list. He couldn't concentrate, though, and his thoughts kept going back to her.

Not in a good way. Over and over, he replayed their last conversation the night he'd left for Chicago, two days before her annual shelter Christmas party. Leaving her to complete the final prep for the party without his help was lame, but he'd had to go that night, for his own peace of mind.

She held parties for the families on Valentine's Day, Easter, Thanksgiving and Christmas. If he'd spent another wonderful holiday with her, he would never have been able to leave. That would've ended with him resenting her for keeping him from his goals. Neither of them would've benefited from that.

Now she was mad. Good and mad and she was his main witness. He doubted she'd relax enough around him to come up with those repressed memories if she had any.

Strike three. He was out.

Enough waiting.

Logan crossed to the harried nurse to ask for an update. He heard Skyler's voice coming from behind a divider, grinding his feet to a halt. He listened as a doctor explained that rest, particularly resting her eyes, would let her brain heal faster from her concussion.

A concussion. Just like Darcie suspected.

Skyler's voice as she thanked the doctor for the quality care and said goodbye cut through his thoughts. The last thing he wanted was for her to think he was spying on her so he took his seat again and pulled out his phone. She stopped at the nurse's desk, but Logan couldn't make out their intense conversation.

When he finally heard her footsteps crossing over to him, he resisted making eye contact. Instead, he continued to thumb through the screens on his phone.

"Logan," she said, now standing over him. "I thought I made it clear that I'd find a ride home."

He looked up, and, though her brows were knitted in irritation, his heart turned over. Seeing her today had unsettled him more than he would've thought possible.

"I wanted to make sure you were okay." He schooled himself to remain detached as he stood. "*Are* you okay?"

"Fine."

"No concussion or other damage?"

"I said I'm fine." She turned away, her tension palpable.

She was unable to face him while dodging his question, which meant she was planning to hide the concussion from him. He opened his mouth to demand she tell him, but he had no right to know about it or anything else in her life. As she'd said, he'd given up that right when he'd walked out. But he wouldn't let her jeopardize her health. He was about to ask more probing questions when Paul Parsons rushed into the lobby, his tie loosened at the neck and a five-o'clock shadow darkening his jaw.

"Good, I'm glad I caught you," he said, sounding out of breath, his microphone conspicuously missing.

Skyler rubbed her forehead. "Now's not a good time for an interview."

"I'm not giving up on the interview, but this isn't about that." Parsons took a gulp of air. "I was outside and Clyde called the station, demanding to speak to me. They patched him through to my cell."

"He what?" Logan asked, wondering what angle Parsons was working here.

"I know. Weird, right?" Parsons's phone chimed, and he dug it out. "He said he saw my story outside the bank on TV and wanted me to pass a message on to Deputy Brennan." He glanced at his phone. "Interesting. Very interesting." He looked at Skyler. "My producer tracked the phone number Clyde called from." He paused and, if possible, Logan knew he'd insert a drumroll here for effect.

"And?" Logan asked, trying to hurry him along.

Parsons turned to Skyler. "The phone's registered to you."

"Me?" Skyler seemed confused.

"He used your cell to call Jake at the bank," Logan said. "Did you realize he kept it?"

"I…hadn't really thought about it."

"I'll have Wagner check the bank and if it's missing he can run a GPS search."

"You'll want to hear this message first." Parsons sounded mad, likely because they hadn't waited with bated breath for the message.

"Go ahead," Logan said.

"Clyde was very specific about what he wanted me to say and made me write it down to get it right." Parsons flipped a few pages on his pad. "He said, and I quote, 'I see the fall didn't do my job for me. When I'm through with you, Deputy, even the best E.R. docs in the world won't be able to save you.'"

"He knows I'm here." Her gaze shot around the space. "Which means he's nearby. Watching." Her focus returned to Logan, fear clouding her eyes.

Logan had spent hours in the lobby and knew for certain that Marty wasn't in the waiting room. But he could be peering at them through the windows. Keeping his body between Skyler and the windows, he pushed her toward the nurses' station.

"What're you doing?" she protested.

He didn't care if she got angry with him for making a decision for her again. He needed to get her out of the lobby before Marty made good on his threat and fired a shot through the window to end her life.

FIVE

The police surrounded the hospital, but Logan didn't feel any better about Skyler's safety. Wagner had tracked her phone via GPS, and they'd found it in a trash can outside the E.R.

Marty had been right there. Not more than a thousand feet from Skyler. And a thousand feet away from Logan arresting the guy. Logan wouldn't let him get this close again. Not unless Logan was slapping cuffs on the guy.

Staying vigilant, he opened the door to the dusky night settling around the hospital. As they'd waited for the police to secure the area, a cold front had swept through, along with driving rain and heavy wind, shaking the hospital windows. The downpour had since let up, and the drastic change in temperature left the night foggy and damp.

"Stay close," he said as he escorted her through the reporters and police officers.

Parsons stood at the far end of the walkway narrating a report. "We're hoping Deputy Brennan will give us her thoughts on this threat Clyde has made on her life. Wait—there she is now. I'll ask her." Parsons burst through the crowd. "Deputy Brennan!" he shouted.

Logan didn't care if he was interfering again. He kept Skyler moving forward, settling her into the car before Parsons reached them. Logan wanted to brush Parsons off, but he couldn't keep doing so without making the guy mad. Something that wouldn't paint the FBI in a good light and wouldn't sit well with Inman.

Logan turned with a well-practiced smile. "If you'll give me your business card, I'll be sure to contact you when we're ready to issue a press release."

Parsons lowered his mic and slashed a hand across his throat for his cameraman. "I was hoping after passing on Clyde's message, Deputy Brennan or you would give me an exclusive interview."

Not happening. "Give me your card, and I'll see what I can do."

Parsons dug a card from his pocket but held it out of reach. "Let's trade."

Logan's irritation was mounting, but moving ahead at the bureau depended on his ability to handle situations like this tactfully. He fished out a temporary card with the local FBI number on it and gave it to Parsons. "Now, if you'll excuse me, Deputy Brennan really needs to get some rest."

"Be sure you call me," he said, handing his card to Logan. "Preferably tonight."

Logan climbed behind the wheel and flicked the card onto the dash. "Have you ever dealt with this guy before?"

"No." Skyler buckled her belt. "But I watch him on the news. He's relentless. I doubt he'll go away willingly."

"Hopefully a bigger story will grab his attention tomorrow." Logan started the car. "Mind putting your address in my GPS?"

She started typing on the keypad as he eased through the parking lot. He used his mirrors to search the inky darkness for any threat. Once he was satisfied they hadn't caught a tail, he relaxed—a little. After all, Marty was still out there somewhere. And he didn't want Skyler to relax, either.

"It's a good idea to remain on alert the next few days," he said.

When she sighed, he glanced at her and found her fingers massaging her head again. He hated to bother her with anything when her head must be splitting, but he'd be remiss if he didn't pursue it. "This is important, Skyler."

She blew out another long breath. "You really think Marty will follow through on his threat?"

"Don't you? Especially after he showed up here with your phone tonight?" he asked without sugarcoating his words in hopes she'd take the threat seriously.

"I did when Parsons told us about the message, but I've had time to think about it. Now I'm less inclined to believe it." She swiveled to face him. "I've been on the FRS for eighteen months now, and I've had my share of death threats. I guess it's understandable. I come into people's lives when they're in crisis. But they soon forget all about me, and I've never had anyone make good on their threats."

"This is different," he said trying to hold his frustration at bay. "Marty's already acted."

"You mean the message?" She lifted her chin. A sure sign she planned to fight his suggestion and prove her independence as she always had. "I learned long ago that people like Marty get their kicks by trying to intimidate others. They like to send texts and letters, and make threatening calls, but rarely follow through. If he's announcing his plans, he's not likely coming after me. Plus, it makes more sense for him to leave town to escape arrest."

"You didn't see the way he glared at you before taking off. He clearly has revenge on the brain, and my experience tells me he'll attempt to kill you. The only question in my mind is when." Logan rolled to a stop at a red light and fired a pointed look at her.

Her gaze didn't waver. "Maybe you're right, and I will be on my guard, but I'm a deputy. I know how to handle myself. I'll do what's necessary to stay safe, but I'll be the judge of what's necessary." After holding his gaze for a moment, she shifted to watch out the window.

Fine. It was going to be that way between them.

He followed the GPS directions to Portland's Pearl District. Warehouses and railroad yards once occupied the area, but now it was known for upscale businesses and expensive residences. Condos hovered around a million dollars. Surely, Skyler's promotion to negotiator didn't provide enough income to rent in this neighborhood, much less purchase one of the many condos. Though questions begged to be asked, he wouldn't embarrass her by doing so.

"It's the old firehouse on the next corner," Skyler said when the GPS voice announced their destination.

He slowed in front of the three-story brick building with massive front columns and bright red doors in the semi-residential neighborhood.

"You really live here?" The question slipped out before he could filter it.

"Yes." The gleam in her eyes said she was enjoying his confusion. "You can park in the driveway."

The building sat back from the road, with a wide driveway lined with pines. As he pulled in, exterior floodlights clicked on, giving him a view of perfectly trimmed shrubs where Marty could easily hide.

Still baffled about the firehouse, he looked at Skyler. "You didn't bring me here to ditch me and hide your real address, did you?"

"No. I live here." She laughed and didn't seem inclined to put him out of his misery.

Before he could check the surroundings, she started for the front door. He planted a hand on his weapon and surveyed the area as he stuck close to her. She flashed him an irritated look. She wanted him to back off. He got it. Loud and clear.

Too bad. He wouldn't risk it.

"You really do live here?" he said to keep her from arguing with him about his nearness.

"Not just me. The whole squad does."

"Still, even with the six of you, I don't see how you can afford it."

She bent to flick on a timer plugged into an outlet, lighting the trees with hundreds of twinkling white lights and flooding the darkness with holiday cheer.

"Wow," he said turning in a circle. "I was just starting to accept that you lived here, but these lights? When did you get so many of them? Some rich relative die and leave you a fortune?"

She dug out her keys. "The lights are mine. Bought them on clearance. The firehouse belongs to the county."

"Okay, now I know you're kidding me. I remember when the city sold this building to a private investor."

"You're right. The Kerr family bought it. Darcie saved Winnie Kerr's life on a callout and she donated the building to the county to thank Darcie."

"I've heard of being grateful, but she just ups and gives away a multimillion-dollar building?"

"Yes." Skyler inserted her key in one of the solid oak doors, where a large pine wreath freshened the air. "Darcie basically adopted Winnie, like she does so many other strays, and they became friends. One day Darcie was commenting about her rent going up again. With the county freezing wages, everyone on the squad was struggling to make ends meet. The Kerrs had recently bought this building and Winnie figured it would be a good way to repay Darcie."

"But why donate it to the county instead of giving it to Darcie directly?"

"Darcie wouldn't accept it." Skyler pushed open the door. "But she did agree to live here if it benefited all of us and future squad members. We really consider this home like the firefighters stationed here did. Except we live here full-time."

She flipped an interior light switch, revealing an open industrial space that had once housed the trucks.

Skyler took a few steps inside and turned. "On this floor, we have a communal kitchen, dining room, family room and even a recreation area and gym. We each have our own condo on the second and third floors. There's an elevator accessible from the back, giving us private entrances to our condos." She plugged in another set of lights. "Or these steps lead there, too."

Garlands with white lights coiled up the black metal banister opening onto a second-floor balcony. A two-story tree loaded with decorations filled the corner.

He whistled at the colorful stack of presents bursting from beneath the lowest boughs. "I guess someone's been good this year."

"They're not for us. I hold the shelter party here now instead of renting a venue."

"Sounds nice."

"It's almost perfect." She dropped her keys in a glass bowl on a long metal table. "And speaking of perfect, wait here while I turn on the other lights so you can get the full effect."

She headed toward the back of the building, quickly disappearing from view. Not happening. He wanted her within sight until he thoroughly checked out the building. After securing the door, he stepped across the polished concrete floor until he could see her again.

She bent next to a spruce that soared toward the ceiling crisscrossed with heavy metal beams. Lights suddenly flooded the tree, reflecting off wall-to-wall windows with curving arches. She stood and flicked a switch by a massive fireplace bringing the room to life.

Perfect, he thought. The perfect Christmas decor to make

up for the dismal holidays she'd hinted at having as a child. Exactly what she strived for every holiday.

"Okay, Logan," she called out. "You can come in now."

When he reached her, she was gently fingering a fragile handmade origami star coated in wax. They'd purchased a set of twelve that last Christmas together. He saw the others spread out on branches and was stunned that she'd actually kept them.

"Remember these?" She turned the star. The light caught the glitter and sparkled over her fingers.

The memory of shopping with her for the ornaments she'd said she'd cherish for a lifetime came whirling back like the snow falling that day. They'd held hands, moving in and out of shoppers in downtown Portland. Her cheeks pink from the cold. Snowflakes glistening in her hair. The pure fun and joy that had been part of his life when they were together.

"I remember." His voice caught at the reminder of all he'd given up when he'd walked away from her. But the professional gain had been worth it, he reminded himself.

She suddenly looked away, but he saw tears shining in her eyes, before she turned.

"How about a tour of the place?" he asked to break the moment between them. "If you're up to it with the head injury and all."

A curtain fell over her eyes, covering her emotions, and he felt bad for ignoring them. He opened his mouth to speak, but she spun on her heel. "If you follow me, I'll show you the kitchen."

Feeling like a jerk, he traipsed behind her. She'd tried to talk to him about their past, maybe bring some resolution to how they'd left things, and he'd shut her down. More important, he'd hurt her once again.

She stopped by a large island overlooking the family

room. "Winnie kept the feel of the firehouse but spared no expense in the remodel. Everything's top-of-the-line."

He took in the bright red metal cabinets, stainless-steel countertops and industrial appliances. Metal air ducts ran along the ceiling, as did water pipes and electrical conduits.

She planted her hands on the island. "Having such a large kitchen helps immensely with prep for the holiday parties."

"Are you still doing all of them?"

She nodded. "Plus, I've added a tea for Mother's Day where the kids make the food and create homemade gifts for their moms."

"Sounds like fun." He meant it. He liked kids. He just didn't have much experience with or time for them.

"You'll probably be more interested in our rec room." She stepped through a wide doorway at the far side of the kitchen and pointed at a sizable dining table. "Obviously, this is the dining room. Winnie made sure we had a large table for all of us when we were together and any friends we might want to invite."

He counted the chairs as they passed, discovering seating for fourteen.

Skyler went through another expansive doorway into a room painted a cheerful yellow. A pool table sat in the middle of the room. A video game station filled one corner, and a round table covered with puzzle pieces took up another.

Logan fingered a piece. "Your teammates don't strike me as the kind of people who'd sit around doing puzzles."

"You're right. We're all adrenaline junkies in our own right. I mean, you couldn't do this job unless you thrived on danger, right? But some of us are more daring than others. Like Cash. He's our bombs expert. He's former Army Delta Force."

"A special ops, guy, huh? He's lived life on the edge then."

"That's putting it mildly," she said, a smile lighting her

face. "He's into extreme sports and auto racing." She shook her head. "Thankfully, we don't all go to that excess. But most of us don't have the patience for puzzles, either. That's Jake's thing. He's very orderly and likes to do them when he's trying to work out a problem."

Logan could relate to the need for order but not the adrenaline-seeking part. He needed predictability in his life. Needed to know he was in control, and pushing the envelope was far from control.

He crossed the room to a wall of shelves filled with books and board games. Another long section held vintage toys.

"Someone a collector?" he asked.

"Archer."

"The other negotiator?"

She nodded. "He grew up in the lap of luxury and had everything imaginable, but his dad didn't believe kids should play. He groomed Archer to take over the family business from the get-go. He never got the toys he wanted, so he's collecting them now."

Logan had a similar upbringing, but he had no desire for toys now. Not even the electronic gadgets that many men wanted today. Unless he could use them on the job. Then he was the first in line at the electronics store.

Otherwise, a waste of money as far as Logan was concerned. "Looks like he's invested a few bucks here."

"He also makes sure there are plenty of toys for the shelter kids every year," she said defensively, and he could tell she cared about this guy.

A pang of jealousy stabbed Logan. Not because she seemed to care about the men on her team, but because Logan had been the one to help her pick out toys in the past.

He went to the arched window facing the front of the house, giving him a spectacular view of the pines spilling light into the darkness. "This is really quite the setup you have here."

"It is and we're thankful for it. We have a lot of stress in our jobs, and this is one place we can actually relax."

At the true joy in her voice, he turned to face her. "Sounds like you really like it here."

"We all do. Either we have family we don't get along with or don't have any family at all. Plus all the others moved here from out of state so we support each other. And since we're all single…" She quickly cut her gaze away.

He suspected she was thinking about where she might be if they'd stayed together.

He heard a car pull up outside, and his hand automatically went for his gun.

"Relax," she said, looking out the window. "That's Darcie's car. The rest of the squad will be hot on her heels."

The acerbic paramedic climbed from a rugged SUV. Moments later, another SUV pulled into the driveway and headlights from yet another vehicle followed.

As Skyler had said, her team was home, and that meant Logan no longer had a reason to remain at her side. He'd head back to his hotel.

Alone. Him and his thoughts. Thoughts filled with wonder over the strength he'd once found to walk out on this woman who was as amazing as he'd remembered.

SIX

Skyler greeted her fellow team members in the entry. They were home. All safe and sound. Her constant support in the face of adversity. She blinked back tears of joy from seeing the people who mattered to her most and made sure to welcome them with a smile so they wouldn't worry about her.

"Okay, people." Jake clapped his hands, all business as usual. "We meet in the family room in five minutes to discuss Skyler's safety and formulate a plan to locate Marty before he acts on his threat. So get something to eat or drink, or take a quick break. Whatever you need, but then I want your full attention."

The team scattered, and Skyler prepared to escort Logan out the door.

He approached Jake before she got to him. "I'd like to join in the meeting if you don't mind."

Skyler wasn't surprised Logan wanted to stay and talk about Marty, but she *was* surprised he actually asked instead of demanding to stay.

"I mind." Jake's dark eyes fixed on Logan.

Skyler had been on the end of such a look many times, and she didn't envy Logan having to deal with her unmovable squad leader when he'd set his mind against something.

Logan didn't so much as bat an eyelash. "I get that you're still miffed at my interference at the bank, but I'm only thinking of Skyler here. We'll be more successful if we co-ordinate our efforts instead of repeating them."

"Coordinate? You planning on offering a protective detail for Skyler?" With Jake's experience in requesting special resources with a tight budget, he likely knew Logan couldn't afford to do so.

Logan didn't back down. "Trust me. I'd provide a detail in a heartbeat, but I don't have justification at this point."

Jake crossed his arms over his team shirt, rumpled after a long day. "That's what I thought."

Frustration flitted through Logan's eyes, but it was so quick Jake likely missed it. Not Skyler. She saw it and everything else Logan was trying to hide.

That was Logan through and through. Stay strong and tough. Never show emotion in public. Never let others see his weaknesses. His FBI father had drilled that into him from his early days. When Skyler was dating him, she'd had to work hard to get him to unwind and express his feelings.

"Trust me, Marsh." Logan planted his feet on the floor and his hands on his hips. "When I have grounds to provide a protective detail, I will. Until that time, we can work together in a less official capacity."

Jake turned to Skyler, his expression softening. "You want him to stay?"

Yes. No. She didn't know. She shrugged. "I'm not sure it matters what I want. Logan tends to do whatever *he* wants to do."

A flicker of pain lit his eyes, but it disappeared as quickly as the frustration.

"I guess that means you can stay," Jake said, but he sounded as if the idea bothered him. "I'm gonna grab a soda."

Skyler smiled her thanks at Jake for his protectiveness.

Carrying drinks and a bag of chips, Cash and Archer stepped into the foyer. She expected them to go straight to the family room, but they must've picked up on the tension flowing between her and Logan and they stopped next to her.

The two of them were like night and day. Cash was sturdy with rippling muscles, while Archer was long and lean, but no less powerful. If they weren't in uniform, their difference would be even more pronounced. Cash often chose his worn Western boots and jeans reflecting his Texas upbringing, while Archer wore khakis and custom-fitted shirts—a holdover from growing up with wealthy parents in New York City.

"You okay, squirt?" Archer asked, eyeing Logan.

As the tallest on the squad, Archer always teased her for her five-six stature. The nickname "squirt" caught on and stuck. Everyone but Darcie used it.

"I'm fine." She tried to smile at him, but from the continued concern in his expression, she hadn't been convincing.

She expected him to fire off an opinion of her best course of action, but he carefully appraised her as Cash stood silently watching them both.

"I'm not buying that you're fine," Archer finally said as he continued to peer at her closely. "But then you already know that. Still, after all you've been through today, I'll cut you some slack."

As the other negotiator on the team, they should have a lot in common, but they didn't. Her degree in psychology made her look deep into people for motives. He held an MBA from Harvard and considered facts and figures. Still, he had a passion for the underdog and thought all people mattered, not just the wealthy and powerful.

"Fair warning, though." He quirked a brow. "Tomorrow's a different story." He winked at her before heading into the family room.

Cash snorted. "Never thought I'd see him back down."

"Guess almost getting killed paid off for once." She tried to chuckle, but it came out flat.

"Hey, squirt." Cash's voice softened, his Southern drawl as smooth as honey. "It'll be okay. I promise."

"How can you promise that?"

"I'm proof." He mocked a model's pose, making her grin for real. "How many times did I almost take a bullet in Afghanistan? I'm still going strong, and you, my friend—" he paused, lifting his hand as if planning to pat her shoulder but then decided against it "—are far tougher than I am."

She caught sight of Logan hovering in her peripheral vision, waiting to swoop in if she needed help. But Cash was family. Even as the newest squad member, he was there for Skyler when she needed him. Something Logan didn't understand.

"You're a real softy. You know that, Cash?" she said.

"Shh." He lifted his finger to his mouth. "Don't let anyone else hear you say that. It'll wreck my cred." Smiling, he left her honestly feeling better about her situation.

Logan wasted no time, but stepped over to her. "Looks like your teammates are good friends."

She took in the group gathering in the other room and her heart swelled over her blessed life. "They're my family."

"I don't want to intrude." The sadness in his tone brought her attention back to him. "I'll leave if you want me to."

"It's fine." Her teammates' tender concern had pushed away her strife for the time being, and she actually was okay with Logan staying. At least for now. "Take a seat in the family room. These meetings tend to go on for hours, so I'm going to put on a pot of coffee."

She didn't wait for a response before heading to the kitchen. She settled the carafe under the refrigerator's dispenser and listened to the gurgle of water. Without all the turmoil taking her focus, she noticed the throbbing pain threatening to split her skull. She rested her head against the cool stainless steel.

"Your head bothering you?" Darcie asked, her tone low and relaxed. Raised in the Florida panhandle, she spoke with a Southern accent, but stress often deepened it like today.

Translated, Darcie was worried about her. Something Skyler appreciated, so she wouldn't blow off her concern with a trite response. "The pain medicine they gave me at the E.R. is wearing off."

Nearly six feet tall, Darcie easily reached the top cupboard and withdrew a first aid kit. She poured two tablets into Skyler's hands. "This'll help with the external pain. Nothing I can do for the heartache I see in your eyes."

Skyler swallowed the acetaminophen without water.

Darcie perched on a stool and crossed long legs that Skyler often envied. "Do you still have a thing for him?"

A denial came to Skyler's lips, but she stopped it. This was Darcie. Her best friend. Best friends helped each other when they were conflicted. "I'm still attracted to him if that's what you're asking."

"Not surprising. He's a good-looking man. It'd be odd if you didn't find him attractive."

"You think he's good-looking, huh?" Skyler winked.

Darcie rolled her eyes. "A girl would have to be blind not to see that, but honestly the fact that he walked out on you the way he did makes him very unappealing to me. It was so selfish. He kind of reminds me of your parents."

Skyler knew he also reminded Darcie of her ex-husband, who had left her after their daughter died in a car accident four years ago, but she refused to talk about him. Ever, and now wouldn't be an exception.

She shook her head. "I'm surprised after the way your family hurt you that you even fell for someone like him."

Skyler's response to Logan baffled her, too, but then the heart wasn't always logical.

"Why aren't you saying anything?" Darcie eyed her. "Is it because you know I'm right and he's the worst possible choice for you?"

Skyler sighed. "Okay, I admit it. You're right. He *is* a lot like my parents, but, in his defense, I know he doesn't want to be that way. He just has this insatiable need to prove his worth to his father."

Darcie's eyebrow quirked up in question. "So you're saying once he does that, he'll change?"

She shrugged. "All I know is that when he's not focused on the job, he's a kind and considerate man."

"Kind and considerate doesn't walk out on you."

"Ignore what he did to me for the moment. He was great with all the shelter families. I saw the genuine joy in his face when he helped them. You can't fake that."

Or can you? A niggling of doubt wormed its way into her brain. It was bad enough that he'd chosen his job over her, but maybe he hadn't ever been the man she'd once thought he was.

"Either way, it's you I'm worried about." Darcie gently poked Skyler's chest. "What's happening in there? Are you letting this guy get to you again? Because if you are, I'm sure you're in for a world of hurt."

That was the six-million-dollar question, and Skyler had no idea if she still had feelings for him. She hoped not, but how could she know? After Darcie's comments, Skyler didn't even know who the real Logan Hunter was inside. Didn't matter, though, did it? She wouldn't open her heart long enough to find out.

SEVEN

Skyler's team hadn't taken their eyes off Logan for the past hour, and he felt like a fish in a public aquarium. He was different than these people—even dressed differently and it took him back to his younger years. He swallowed down memories of his father. Memories that made him vow never to let other's opinions of him matter again. To focus on concrete actions. Actions he and others around him could use to gauge his success. After all, wasn't that what dear old dad wanted.

So why did he want Skyler's friends to like him? To realize that he'd never wanted to hurt her?

He couldn't accomplish that and shut them down at the same time. He hadn't lied to Jake when he'd said he wanted to coordinate their efforts, but he wanted the team to focus on protecting Skyler, not on finding Marty. The only way he'd arrest Marty by the arbitrary deadline set by Inman was to control every step of this investigation.

So despite this unexpected desire to be liked, he pushed off the fireplace mantel where he'd been resting his shoulder.

"I appreciate all of your suggestions," he said, trying to sound grateful for their efforts. "But I can't have any of you interfering in my investigation. Every step will be carefully calculated and one false move could throw us off course."

Cash glared up at Logan from his seat in a leather club chair. "We're all trained in investigative techniques. I assure you we'll be discreet and won't step on your toes, Suit."

"My name's Logan. Or Agent Hunter if you prefer. Not Suit." Logan returned Cash's hard stare with one of his own. "Given enough time I suspect you would locate Marty, but you can't mount an unsanctioned investigation, and I'm not opposed to arresting anyone who tries."

Cash came to his feet. Thrusting out his chest, he approached Logan. Logan pulled back his shoulders and prepared for a showdown that he fully intended to win.

"C'mon, guys." Skyler stepped between them. The top of her head barely came up to their chins, but Cash obviously knew not to mess with her as he backed away.

"I know everyone wants to get Marty off the street." She turned to the others. "But that's Logan's job and we have to respect that."

Logan flashed a grateful smile at her, but she didn't acknowledge it. "If this was any other standoff and Marty hadn't threatened me, you'd already have put it behind you. Sure, maybe you'd have a passing interest in the investigation, but you wouldn't be trying to insert yourself in the middle of it. Let's do the right thing here. Let Logan handle the robbery investigation."

"But Marty *did* threaten you, and you're family," Cash argued. "We don't leave family members in danger, Skyler. Not without trying to stop it."

Logan didn't fault him for that sentiment at all. "I'm fine with all of you taking steps to protect Skyler. In fact, I encourage a 24/7 detail to ensure her safety."

"Let's not go overboard here, okay?" Skyler flashed him a frustrated look. "A round-the-clock detail isn't necessary. Marty hasn't tried anything. He simply spouted off and sent a message. Besides, I can take care of myself."

Right. Her independent streak. Something in her past

made it hard for her to let anyone help her. She'd never explained it, but Logan knew standing on her own two feet was her go-to response.

Jake stood, stretching to his full height. "Suit's right. I'll work on a schedule tonight to make sure one of us is with Skyler at all times, starting right now."

"No," Skyler insisted. "We all have our regular jobs to do. If we change schedules before finding proper replacements, we'll put the public at risk. I won't let that happen. Especially when it's not necessary."

"Regular jobs?" Logan asked.

Skyler nodded. "The county can't support a full-time strategic response unit. Other than Jake, we work in various departments and we're on call for crisis incidents. Cash is on river patrol, Brady's with search and rescue. Archer's a community resource officer and Darcie's a paramedic."

"And you?"

"I'm still a detective with the Special Investigations Unit."

"Which means," Jake said, "I don't have other responsibilities. I'll take the protective detail tomorrow until I can arrange for coverage for everyone else. Does that work for you, Skyler?"

She let out a resigned sigh. "I can't stop you once you've made up your mind, so I'll go along with it. But can you at least be discreet at the office? The last thing I need is for my fellow detectives to harass me about requiring a bodyguard."

Jake snorted, and the others joined in his laugher. Even Brady, who'd been whittling away on a piece of wood, not seeming to pay attention, chuckled.

Logan liked to laugh, too. Okay, maybe not all the time, but he found no humor here. Not when Skyler could be in danger. Besides, she had a concussion. She shouldn't even be going to the office, let alone working a demanding detective's job.

Logan wished he didn't have to clip her wings, but he would for her own good. "Did the doctor clear you to go to work tomorrow? What with the concussion and all?"

"Concussion?" Darcie shot to her feet and crossed to Skyler. She tipped up Skyler's head and peered into her eyes. "You didn't say a word about a concussion. Were you planning to hide it from us?"

Skyler jerked her chin free. "It's no big deal."

"May not be." Jake appraised them both. "But consider yourself on leave until you receive written clearance to return to duty."

For the first time today, Logan was on the other man's side.

"Relax, okay?" Skyler waved a dismissive hand in the air. "I feel fine."

"Concussions are nothing to take lightly," Darcie said, her focus still on Skyler. "The brain is sensitive. Healing isn't only a matter of taking it easy so you don't further jar your brain. It's also about letting the brain rest. You need to stay away from things that require strong focus. From overwhelming sounds, bright lights, et cetera. And that means staying away from work. If you don't, your healing will take longer."

"Yeah, what she said," Jake added. "Plus, as your supervisor, I insist on following protocol."

"Right." Cash drew the word out in his Texas drawl as his eyes lit with humor. "Because you wouldn't want to make an exception to the rules even one time. Who knows, we could have a major case of anarchy if you did."

Jake cast him a cool look. "This isn't the time for one of your unconventional opinions, Cash. This is about Skyler's health."

"Right, her health." Cash smirked. "*And* the rules."

Brady snorted. "Good one, bro."

"I second that," Archer weighed in for the first time tonight.

"Maybe we could compromise," Skyler interjected. "Since I was involved in the bank standoff from the hostage side, I believe I can offer valuable information at the team debrief in the morning. Let me attend that meeting. Then I'll come home, put my feet up right here and stare at my garden for the rest of the day."

"You won't drive," Jake warned. "I'll give you a ride to the office."

"I can bring her back home afterwards," Darcie offered. "That'll give me plenty of time to assess how she's doing when she can't run away from me."

Skyler groaned, but Logan could see fondness for her teammates in her expression.

"Who'll man the protective detail once she gets home?" Logan asked.

Jake looked at Logan. "Don't worry your pretty-boy head. I'll figure something out."

Archer stood and checked his watch. "We should wrap this up." He retucked his uniform shirt and adjusted his belt. "We're all tired from the stress of seeing our little squirt in danger."

"And we're hungry." Brady rubbed his stomach before kicking down the leg support on his recliner. "Whose night is it to cook anyway?"

"Mine," Cash muttered.

"Say it ain't so," Brady said, the word *so* coming out in two syllables of Midwest twang.

Everyone groaned, and Logan felt a smile tug at his mouth.

"Please, someone do something quick." Darcie grinned, and Logan could see she was a real beauty when she wasn't worried or defensive. "Skyler's already nauseous from the head injury. She can't possibly eat Cash's cooking. Someone else should volunteer."

"Guess that means you're up, Darcie." Cash flashed a satisfied smile. "At least according to Jake's house rules."

Jake nodded. "He's right. He who complains the loudest fixes the problem."

"I really hate going to work," Skyler said with a snide smile.

"Nice one." Darcie slapped a high five with Skyler.

"Just don't expect it to change my mind." Jake gestured at the kitchen. "C'mon, Darcie. I'll help you feed this ungrateful bunch."

The group broke up and as soon as they'd left the room, Logan missed their good-natured interaction. They were a real team. The kind that could achieve anything together. He was glad they were part of Skyler's life.

He approached her to say good-night. She was staring after Jake as if she didn't really understand his approach to life.

"I take it Jake's a by-the-rules kind of guy," Logan said.

"You have no idea. He's all about the job and controlling everything around him. He doesn't have a social life. Lives like a hermit." She laughed, then suddenly sobered. "Come to think of it, you do have an idea what's he's like, don't you, Logan? A very good one."

As Skyler had said, Logan had a good idea of Jake's life. He'd only known Jake for a day but he recognized the same focus and intensity that Logan himself lived by. That's why he still sat behind a desk at the FBI office at ten o'clock that night. Jake was probably working, too. But Logan wasn't Jake. Far from it. Jake surrounded himself with team members who invested in each other's lives. Not just professionally, but personally. Logan hadn't had anyone who was truly invested in his life since Skyler.

Skyler.

What was he going to do about her?

She wouldn't acknowledge the danger she was in. Though a free spirit, she was also headstrong when she wanted to be. He could see her convincing her teammates that she'd be fine on her own. See them going about life and leaving her alone. Marty swooping in. Taking her life.

The sick feeling that had lingered since he'd seen her on the monitors that afternoon intensified. When they'd been a couple, he'd cared more for her than any woman he'd ever known, and he hadn't left her because he'd lost interest or didn't care. He'd walked away because he'd had no choice. Following his dream meant going to Chicago—and leaving her behind.

None of it her fault.

He shouldn't have gotten involved with her—anyone for that matter—when he still had so much to do. But he hadn't been able to resist her and she'd ended up being the one good and decent thing in his life.

Until he'd ended it. Badly.

Now he owed her his best to make sure Marty didn't harm her.

He couldn't leave her protection up to her squad until he confirmed there were no loopholes in the schedule and that she hadn't convinced them to relax. He had some juggling to do to run the investigation and meet his deadline, while at the same time making sure she was safe.

On his phone, he opened the message group he'd set up for his team.

Daily briefing changed to 6:00 a.m. Effective immediately, he typed. Confirm your availability.

He sent the text and sat back to wait for their responses. Even if the whole team couldn't attend, Logan would keep to this schedule, freeing him up for daily check-ins with Skyler.

He imagined showing up on her doorstep tomorrow morning. She'd plant her fists on her hips while jutting out her cute little chin. Her eyes would narrow and she'd look like an adorable pit bull as she told him in no uncertain terms that she was in charge of her life and he didn't need to horn in.

He had to find a way to gain her agreement. And maybe after that, he'd explain his reasons for leaving. They'd talk about it and reach an agreement to put their past behind them to keep it from distracting them.

Yes, that was what he had to do. Somehow.

Because if he knew one thing, it was that distractions could be dangerous when you were hunting down a killer. Almost as dangerous as the killer.

EIGHT

Logan laid on his horn to move the melee of reporters out of the way as he maneuvered into the firehouse drive. He spotted Parsons lurking near one of the large bay doors painted a vivid red, his microphone clasped in his hand as usual. When the reporter spied Logan, his face lit with excitement.

Great way to start the morning.

Groaning, Logan jogged toward the main entrance. Parsons trailed after him.

Logan pounded on the door and tapped his foot as he waited. "C'mon, c'mon, c'mon. Someone answer."

The door jerked open. Jake, wearing the black team uniform again, blocked Logan from entering.

Logan gestured at the reporters. "Can I come in before the mob gets to me?"

"Hmm," Jake said, looking over Logan's shoulder.

"C'mon, man," Logan begged. "I know you're not thrilled with me, but reporters? That's an extreme punishment for yesterday, isn't it?"

Jake chuckled and moved out of the way.

Logan slipped past him and closed the door in Parsons's face. "Thanks, man. You saved my hide." Logan mocked an exaggerated shudder.

Jake's grin disappeared as he twisted the dead bolt. "I assume you're here to see Skyler."

Logan nodded. "But I also want to review her protection schedule."

"I'm still working on it." Jake's narrowed eyes fixed on Logan. "I need to talk to other department heads before I can finalize assignments."

"When can I take a look at it?"

Jake took a solid stance. "I don't recall saying you can."

Relax, Logan warned himself. *Or you'll be butting heads with this guy all the time.*

"Sorry, man. The detail is your thing and I'll respect that. It's just…" Logan paused for a moment, wondering if he should head down this path. "Skyler and I…we…we have a history, you know? And I need to make sure she'll be okay."

"Trust me—we know all about your history." Jake crossed his arms and widened his stance. "And we won't appreciate it if you hurt her again."

"That's not my intent."

"See that it's not or you'll have five extremely angry people with guns to deal with." Jake quirked a smile, but his tone was deadly serious.

"So where is she?"

"Out back. In her garden."

"Thanks for letting me in." Logan turned toward the back of the house.

"Don't make me regret it," Jake called after Logan.

He stepped outside and took a moment to appreciate the sun shining down on three tiers of boulders holding back the earth. A variety of plants cascaded over the rocks, most of the foliage brown and crumbly. Logan remembered Skyler's love of gardening, but she'd only had a small terrace with potted plants when they were together. All he knew about plants was that they were either green or brown and he didn't know which they should be at this time of year.

She looked up, her hands filled with long blades of decorative grass she'd been snipping. "What're you doing here?"

Her blatant suspicion made him cringe. She didn't trust him anymore. Might never trust him again, and he hadn't a clue how to fix it other than to explain himself and ask her forgiveness.

"Well?" She dumped the grass in a bucket and crossed her arms over the black hoodie she wore with a vintage paisley blouse. "You didn't say why you were here," she said more pointedly.

"I was worried about you."

"No need." She slipped her clippers into a green gardening apron strung around her narrow waist. "I still have a headache, but otherwise I'm fine."

"I'm glad to hear that, but I was talking more about your safety." He took a few steps closer, earning a testy look.

"Jake's here."

"I know, it's just…" He turned away until he found the right words to express himself. "We once meant a lot to each other, and I need to personally make sure Marty doesn't harm you." She opened her mouth. He knew a refusal was coming, so he rushed on. "After the way I ended things between us, I don't deserve any consideration. I get that. Trust me. You've made that perfectly clear."

She shoved her hands in the pockets of well-worn jeans. "And yet you're here."

The bitterness in her tone made him want to drop the subject, but he held his ground. "I thought maybe you'd let me drive you to your office and on the way we can clear the air between us. Doesn't look like this case is going away quickly, and we'll be seeing more of each other. Wouldn't it be better if we weren't distracted by our past and could focus on the case? On your safety, too?"

"I'm not distracted."

"C'mon, Skyler." He watched her for any sign of acquiescence. "Your anger with me is obvious."

She jerked a hand out of her pocket and rubbed the back of her neck.

At her indecision, he stepped closer. "I'm sure there are things you want to say to me. And I have things I want to tell you, too. Let's take the time to do it today. Before this case heats up."

"I don't know," she said, but he could tell she was caving.

"Letting this go will only make life better for both of us."

She sighed. "Fine. I'll ride to the office with you, but then you've got to back off."

"I understand," he assured her.

"No." She shook her head. "Don't just 'understand.' Promise you'll back off."

Not something he could do. Ever. "You know I can't, but I *can* promise after I review Jake's schedule, I'll trust your squad to protect you. If they're unavailable or if any attempt is made on your life, I'll be right by your side. That's not negotiable. If that means we can't talk this morning, then that's what has to happen."

She bit her lip. "It's a start, I suppose."

"Enough of a start for you?"

She gave an abbreviated nod. "I'll put my tools away, then tell Jake you're driving me."

"Let me help." He reached for a large bucket filled with dried clippings. He expected her to jerk it away, but she let him carry it to an outdoor storage shed.

"I assume your plants are supposed to be brown." He dumped the bucket in a large recycling bin.

She eyed him, and he could see she was remembering how ignorant he'd been of gardening. "Yes. They're dormant right now, but they're perennials. They'll come back in the spring."

With that, she removed her apron and gloves, shooed

him out of the shed and marched to the sliding glass door. Inside, she went into a room he hadn't seen last night, and he soon heard muffled voices. Jake sounded annoyed. Her voice was strong and determined. Not that Logan was surprised. She might be a little bit of a package on the outside, but she was a strong woman through and through.

As Logan waited, he glanced down the hall at the tree. Sunlight caught on an origami star, sending reflections dancing on the wall. Memories of buying the ornaments once again raced across his mind. The desire for another simple day, shared with a woman he cared about, trailed behind.

How did he reconcile this drive to succeed with this... this what? Longing? Could it even be reconciled or was he destined to live his life driven to succeed at all costs?

And just what are those costs? he asked himself for the first time.

Skyler returned, thankfully saving him from his crazy introspection that would get him nowhere.

Eyes narrowed, she grabbed her purse. "Let's get out of here."

"Something wrong?" He trailed her to the door.

"No," she said, but then he heard her mumble, "Not if people would start minding their own business and let me live my life." She jerked open the door.

"Wait." He rushed to head her off and ensure no threat waited outside. By the time he caught up, she'd stepped out and Parsons had his microphone shoved in her face.

"I'm sorry," she said to the eager reporter. "But I'm late for a meeting."

She tried to sidestep him, but he grabbed the arm already bruised by Marty. She cried out in pain and Logan instantly saw red. Bright, brilliant, fire-engine red.

He didn't even think before he yanked Parsons up by the lapel of his leather jacket and slammed him against the brick. "You lay a hand on her again and you'll wish you hadn't." Logan scowled at him.

"Really?" Parsons lifted his microphone. "What exactly do you plan to do? Maybe use your influence as an FBI agent to stop me?"

His mention of the bureau suddenly cleared Logan's rage, and he looked around. He'd been caught on camera threatening and accosting a reporter. He'd made a mistake. A huge one. One that might jeopardize the ASAC job.

He released Parsons. "I would never use my professional connections for any such thing. Deputy Brennan sustained an injury in the arm you grabbed, and I needed to stop you before she suffered even more. Now if you'll excuse me." He straightened his suit jacket, then turned to Skyler. "Let's roll."

As he moved toward the car, he heard Parsons discussing police brutality. Logan suppressed the urge to turn around and show him what brutality might actually look like.

In the car, Skyler sighed. "Why do some reporters have to be such jerks?"

"That was all my fault. I lost my cool. I shouldn't have."

"I agree," she said. "You shouldn't have lost it, but I appreciate you defending me."

"You do?" He stared at her, his mouth hanging open, before he thought to close it. "I figured you'd be telling me to mind my own business again."

"This was different. You weren't butting in or speaking for me. You were being chivalrous."

"Chivalrous?" The surprise he felt lingered in his voice. "I'm the first to admit I'm not a knight in shining armor."

"When you put your focus in the right place, you're a wonderful knight," she said sadly, then stared out the window.

Baffled by her mixed messages, Logan started the car and carefully merged into traffic. An awkward silence settled around them, and he suspected she was thinking about her knight comment.

He'd like to have the qualities of a knight. To be valiant, honorable—and unwaveringly loyal. To her or any woman. He was sure he possessed the capacity for that kind of loyalty. And he'd prove it…someday. Once he'd gotten to where he wanted to be in life and had time to focus on a relationship.

He opened his mouth to apologize to her, but the words lodged in his throat. How did he start this very important conversation when he knew going to Chicago had been the correct decision? He wouldn't lie to her about that. Could he somehow convey his remorse at hurting her while making it clear that he still needed to keep his focus on his career?

"I thought you wanted to talk," she finally said.

Might as well just launch into it. "I'm sorry, Skyler. For hurting you, I mean. I hope you can forgive me." He took a breath. "I shouldn't have left you with the party only days away…my timing was so bad. There was too much to do to leave you on your own."

She shot him a surprised look before her eyes narrowed. "So what you're saying is you're not sorry for leaving me—you're just sorry about the timing."

"No… Wait. That's not it." He paused until he could stop at a red light and give all of his focus to her. "I'm sorry about hurting you. Sincerely sorry. I've never made my career goals a secret, but in hindsight, I can see that my work taking precedence came as a big surprise to you."

She crossed her arms. "It might not have if you'd discussed the job opportunity before you took it."

"You're right. I'm sorry for that, as well."

She watched him, and he felt as if she could see every thought zinging through his mind. It made him feel as vulnerable as his father's judgment often had.

"You also could've mentioned sometime in the year we

were together," she continued, "that you thought a long-term relationship would interfere with your career plans. If you'd been honest with me from the start, then I would've known where we stood and I wouldn't have fallen for you."

"I'm sorry," he said again, though he knew it didn't change anything. "Some people can have a relationship and still achieve their goals, but it's looking like I'm not one of those people."

Skyler slid closer to the window, moving as far away from him as possible and withdrawing into herself. He'd botched it. Made things worse. The opposite of what he'd hoped to accomplish.

A horn sounded behind them, and he started through the green light.

"Skyler," he said, hoping she'd let him explain.

She didn't respond, just tightened her arms and stared out the window.

He'd give her a few minutes to sort out her thoughts while he came up with a way to restart the conversation. But restart it, he would. And this time…he'd get it right. He had to. He doubted he'd ever get another chance.

Skyler tried to focus on the passing scenery and ignore Logan's awkward apology, but it rolled through her mind in haunting waves. She'd foolishly let herself hope he'd changed. Why she'd even considered it, she had no idea.

Every step, every move he made confirmed his priorities.

Not everything. He took time out of his busy day to drive you to the office today.

So what?

He'd likely done so because he wanted her cooperation on the investigation so he could find Marty faster. Gain his promotion faster. Prove he was the man he thought he needed to be faster. When all he needed was to let go of the superficial drive and embrace the man she knew him to be. Caring. Kindhearted. Responsible.

All the things she'd want in a man. *If* she wanted a man. Which she didn't, right?

Right.

Still, her attraction to him made her do stupid things. She couldn't afford to be stupid. It only brought additional heartache. It'd taken her two years to get over him, and she wasn't about to let him destroy her life again.

Remember that when he trains that magnetic gaze on you.

Remember your parents.

Their bickering. The unhappiness. The constant struggle to make more money. To get more things. Like Logan. True, he wasn't doing it for the money. He was doing it to feel better about himself, which was likely even more of a motivator to stay the course than her parents' need for things had been. She shoved him out of her mind and replaced him with the warning.

Remember, Skyler. Remember.

NINE

Logan glanced at Skyler. She'd spent the past ten minutes huddled near the door, and he felt the tension rolling off her. Her wounded expression was far worse than any feisty argument they might be having.

"We have to talk about this, Skyler," he said.

She didn't respond.

"Please."

She moved a mere fraction, but he felt her gaze on him. He glanced at her to find her eyes sad and tortured.

"What is it?" he asked.

"My parents," she said so softly he had to strain to hear her. "They're just like you. Work came first. Every single day. I was last. In everything, really—I was never considered more important than work and social climbing. I hated it, but it was the way it was."

She looked away again and her pain cut through him like a machete. She'd never told him much about her family, just that they weren't close. He hadn't pried because he didn't want her digging into his dysfunctional family. He should have. Then he would've known that leaving for his job was the worst thing he could've done to her and tried harder to soften the blow.

Unable to concentrate on his driving when she was so distraught, he pulled to the side of the road and faced her.

"I'm sorry, sweetheart. Leaving the way I did hit you where you're most vulnerable, which was never my intention." He gently turned her by the shoulder to face him and left his hand resting there to transmit his sincerity. "I really am sorry. No wonder you're still angry with me."

She seemed to lean into his hand for a moment before shrugging it off. "I forgave you a long time ago, Logan, and I'm not angry anymore."

"You could've fooled me."

"I'm hurt," she said in a sad little whisper. "Still hurt. That's a whole lot different than angry."

Logan heard the gut-wrenching anguish under her words and he didn't know how to respond. He'd learned early on that life was filled with pain, but now he could grasp how much of the same anguish she'd overcome in her own life.

"I'm amazed you're not still mad at me." His words sounded so trite, but sharing his feelings was a foreign concept to him.

"I have no other choice." Her tone was resigned. "My parents have spent most of their lives being angry with each other over every little thing. Life is too short to repeat that behavior myself."

She'd always been so good at living one day at a time. Keeping her peace in the face of adversity. Until he'd ruined it.

"I know this may not help." He took her hand. "But if the Chicago job hadn't come up, I'd still be here. We'd be together."

"Really?" She pulled her hand free. "I doubt it. Something else would've come along that you'd decide was more important than me or any relationship."

"I really do want someone in my life," he said as convincingly as he could.

"So you say, but actions speak louder than words, Logan."

She was right. As much as he hated hurting her and the jerk that it made him, he still believed that leaving had been the right thing, the only thing he could do at the time.

And she deserved his complete honesty no matter how much it hurt. "You're right. It's not the right thing for me now, but I'm almost there. After I'm promoted to ASAC, I'll be more open to things other than the job." He explained his real reason for being in Portland.

She stared a hole right though him. "You honestly believe when you get this promotion you'll change, don't you?"

"Yeah, why shouldn't I? I'll have proved my father wrong, and then I can move on."

"What if your dad isn't impressed? What if you need to work toward another goal to prove your worth to him?"

"That won't happen," he said adamantly. "I'll be one of the youngest agents ever to become an ASAC. Three full years younger than Dad when he got the job. He'll be impressed. He has to be."

"From everything you say about him, I doubt you can count on it." She clutched his arm as if desperate to convince him. "Let this thing with your dad go. It's already cost you so much."

"Easier said than done."

"You once believed God could help you with this problem. You even said you were making progress in putting everything else aside and trusting Him."

Logan had forgotten that. Forgotten how during their time together he'd relinquished so much of his struggle to God and found some measure of peace.

So when had he stopped letting God take charge?

Easy answer. When the job came up in Chicago. He'd wanted it so badly, he hadn't even thought about God's will. He just quit listening and went back to his old ways. Took control of everything again. Made decisions for himself.

It wasn't a conscious decision, but one that he now recognized that he'd made.

Skyler lifted her chin and firmly met his gaze. "You gave up on God, didn't you? Decided to go it alone again."

He'd done just that. Was still doing it now. Doing what he'd been taught to do. Make goals to reach for. Climb the ladder. Achieve. Make his dad proud.

He'd lived for that—only that—for so long.

Until Skyler entered his life. Beautiful. Soft, sweet Skyler looking up at him with such hope for him burning in her eyes. Hope that he could be the man she wanted him to be. That he'd learn to relax and let go. To live fully as she did.

He was tempted to cling to her hope. To let go. To do as she wished.

You'll never amount to anything. His father's words shot into his head from the day he'd told him he wanted to become a teacher. *Teaching's for someone who can't do anything else.* He'd stared down his nose at Logan. *Guess I should've expected it from you, though. You never were tough enough to run with the big dogs.*

The words, still as painful today as they'd been back then, blotted out Skyler sitting next to him. Blotted out a need to find that elusive peace.

There was plenty of time for that, but his goals had time limits.

That meant he was about to disappoint her again. He didn't want to do so, but he had to.

"The job is at my fingertips, Skyler. I have to go for it," he said, working hard to ignore the way the emptiness in his soul grew. And if that wasn't enough to set his gut burning, he couldn't quit wondering if he was making a mistake. A big mistake.

Skyler climbed from the car and stowed her emotions before she stepped inside the sheriff's office where Darcie would start asking questions. Logan escorted her to the side door. He walked crisply, purposefully, his dress shoes clipping on the concrete. He was on full alert for an attack. She picked up on his anxiety, and every change in their surroundings grabbed her attention.

The wind. The trees. A white paper bag blowing across the parking lot.

Each flicker of movement hinted at danger lurking out of sight, pumping adrenaline through her veins until she reached the entrance and slid her security fob over the electronic lock.

The door clicked open, and a sense of relief washed through her as she turned to him. "Thanks for the ride. You can get back to your job now."

"I'm not leaving until I personally turn you over to your squad."

She rolled her eyes at his overprotectiveness.

He planted his feet. "I'm serious, Skyler. I'm coming in with you."

She was mentally exhausted from their conversation and it wasn't worth the effort to argue, so she held the door open for him.

Together they moved through the busy bull pen area. Her associates looked up from their desks, but other than a quick glance, they didn't speak. Jake wound his way toward them while the rest of the squad sat around the conference room table, waiting for the morning debrief to start.

"I've been here for ten minutes already. I was starting to get concerned," Jake said, but his tone held less of a bite than when he'd argued with her at the firehouse. "Since you insisted on coming over here, Suit, how about giving us an update on the investigation before you take off?"

"Sure," Logan said congenially when Skyler had expected him to ask Jake to quit calling him Suit.

Logan's phone rang and he glanced at it. "It's the Portland SAC. I'll need to take his call first. I'll try to make it quick."

Logan took a few steps away, and Jake went into the conference room. Skyler started to follow, but she heard Inman's raised voice coming through Logan's phone, stopping her.

"Seriously, Hunter?" Inman shouted. "What part of assaulting a reporter says you're ready for the ASAC job?"

Logan tugged at his tie and looked up. He caught her watching and moved farther down the hallway. "Parsons grabbed Sky—Deputy Brennan's injured arm. I had to do something before he hurt her again."

Skyler could no longer make out Inman's words, but she didn't have to hear the man to know Logan was receiving a lecture for shoving and threatening Parsons.

A perfect end to their conversation in the car. If Logan hadn't already decided he needed to forgo everything else in his life to focus on the job, he was sure to do so now that the ASAC job was in jeopardy.

Even if she was foolish enough to think he might care about her, he'd never give up this quest to prove himself.

Remember, Skyler. Remember.

TEN

"So what if he grabbed Brennan?" Inman's pointed question hung in the air, and Logan looked around, searching for a logical response but came up empty.

"Fortunately for you," Inman went on before Logan had to respond. "Brennan could bring Parsons up on assault charges, and Parsons hopes not filing charges against you will keep her at bay. Doesn't mean he won't do a hatchet job on us in the media, though."

"What if I met with Parsons and made nice? Maybe offered an exclusive interview," Logan suggested, though he hated the thought of offering a reward to Parsons for manhandling Skyler.

"That could go a long way in appeasing his anger."

"And your anger? Will it help with that?"

"No, but it'll keep you in the running for the job. For now anyway. Make another rookie mistake like this again and I might not be as lenient." He paused, rapid breathing filtering through the phone. "We clear, Hunter?"

"Clear, sir," he said quickly before he made Inman angrier.

"Fine. Then make this complaint go away. Now!"

Logan hung up and loosened the knot of his tie so he could breathe. He felt like Inman's demands were choking him, but it was Logan's job to make the man happy. He should call Parsons right now, but he needed to cool down first or he'd make things worse. Besides, the team was expecting an update and keeping his word with Jake was important, too.

Or maybe you're not ready to leave Skyler yet, the thought came unbidden.

He ignored it and joined the team in the conference room. All heads snapped in his direction. He'd have to be blind to miss the continued doubt burning in their eyes.

They didn't trust him. Just like Skyler. He'd done things over the years that he wasn't proud of, but he'd always been a man of his word and someone others could count on. Until now.

"What's he doing here?" Darcie asked, her tone openly antagonistic.

"Relax." Jake held up his hands. "I asked him to give us an update." Jake gestured at the head of the table. "Floor's all yours."

Feeling their gazes tracking his every move, Logan forced his head back into the game. "As I mentioned at dinner last night, we were unable to enhance the video to get clear details on Marty's ring, so my team is compiling pictures for Skyler to look at. We hope to have something ready to view later today." Logan turned to Skyler. "I'm assuming I can find you at home to show it to you."

She nodded. "Since my phone will be sitting in evidence for the unforeseeable future, I need to get a new one. Aside from that, I'll be going straight home after we're done here."

"Is Darcie still planning on driving you?" Logan tried to sound curious, but it came out demanding.

Darcie crossed her arms and a flare of irritation sparked in her eyes. "Before you complain that I'm not a cop, I've lived with these guys for years and they've made sure I know how to handle a gun and carry it with me at all times."

"She can at least hit the broad side of a barn." Brady

looked up from a fresh pile of woodchips and winked at Darcie.

She slapped her hand at him, but Logan could see the charming Brady had her wrapped around his finger. Logan personally didn't see the attraction. Brady might be a bundle of energy, always tapping his foot or whittling away at a chunk of wood, but Logan had pegged the guy's attitude as easygoing and carefree. Odd how Logan found the same traits enchanting in Skyler, but they grated on him coming from Brady.

Brady ducked away from Darcie. "Don't blame the messenger. I'm telling the truth."

Darcie wrinkled her nose and seemed to relax.

"I wish you'd sugarcoat something just once in your life." Her lips turned up in a generous smile.

"Ha!" Archer said. "Not possible with him."

Logan watched the teammates, laughing and tossing out more jabs. He couldn't stop feeling like he still didn't fit in. Since he'd met this squad, he'd been thinking they were like a family, but they weren't just like one. They *were* a family. Caring about each other. Teasing. Calling each other out on their faults, yet supporting each other. Like the family he'd wanted growing up.

"Okay, guys," Jake interrupted. "Let's focus so Skyler can go home and get some rest."

Listen to the guy for once.

Logan turned to his task and wrote *makeup* on the whiteboard. "We've analyzed the makeup used to create the prosthetics. It appears to be a professional brand used in theater and films."

"Meaning one of them might be a makeup artist as you suspected," Jake offered.

Logan nodded. "Their robbery spree started in Los Angeles. If they're L.A. residents with a background in makeup, then they likely have a connection to the Hollywood studios. Agents at our field office are showing the prosthetics around to see if anyone knows a makeup artist named Nicole with a boyfriend named Marty or vice versa."

"Sounds like a promising lead," Jake said. "*If* they're actually from L.A."

"Sounds more like a wild-goose chase to me." Brady paused with his knife in midair. "There's gotta be a ton of makeup artists in Hollywood."

Logan didn't want to get into an argument about the merits of his investigation, so he went on. "We're also tracking down local makeup suppliers in case the makeup was purchased in Portland and processing forensic evidence from the scene. We recovered fibers and hair from Nicole, Faith and Skyler's clothing. That, along with Marty's blood from the alley, has been sent to the FBI lab in Quantico for analysis with a request to rush it."

"Sounds to me like you're coming up short on solid leads." Cash eyed Logan. "And you could use some help in the investigation."

"We have things covered," Logan said, trying not to snap.

Skyler sat forward. "Maybe Cash is right."

"I'm always right, squirt." Cash winked at her. "And it's about time someone admitted it around here."

"Puh-lease." Darcie rolled her eyes, then looked at Skyler. "What do you think he's right about?"

"Maybe I was wrong last night and we *should* help in the investigation." Logan opened his mouth to respond, but Skyler rushed on. "Specifically, I mean *I* should help. I have the highest closure rate in my department, so I'd like to think I have strong investigative skills."

"You're on medical leave," Darcie reminded her.

"Plus, your supervisor in the Special Investigative Unit will nix it, anyway," Jake added. "And you have zero justification to work a robbery falling under the FBI's jurisdiction."

"Fine," Skyler said. "Internal Affairs is investigating as they always do when an officer fires a weapon. I could work the case under the guise of helping them."

Brady shook his head. "They don't care about the robbery. They're only concerned about making sure I followed protocol. Since I did, the investigation will be over as fast as it started."

She cast a pleading look at Logan and he was hard-pressed to find a reason to deny her help. Or maybe deny spending more time with her.

Was it possible she didn't care about the investigation and wanted to spend time with him, too?

Daydream, Hunter. A big fat daydream.

It didn't matter anyway. He had no right to consider anything with Skyler unless he could make the kind of commitment she deserved. That he couldn't—wouldn't—do. No matter how much the sparkling blue eyes pleading with him made him want to say yes.

He'd make sure she was safe—that she could count on him—but the investigation had to remain his top priority.

Skyler felt Darcie watching her from the driver's seat, but she ignored her friend's questioning gaze and thumbed through the screens on her new phone. As the self-professed "mom" of the group, Darcie had to be itching to ask about Skyler's ride into the office with Logan, but, honestly, she was still too raw from her earlier discussion with Logan to rehash it with anyone. Even with her best friend.

Skyler stared out the window at the misty rain blanketing the city. In the side mirror, she caught sight of an older-model red Jeep racing toward their bumper with no signs of slowing.

Good. A much-needed distraction. She grabbed her phone and dialed dispatch to report the car's reckless driving. If there was a unit in the area, they'd pull the driver over before he or she hurt anyone. As Skyler talked with dispatch, she glanced in the mirror to catch the license number. She didn't see a plate on the front—possibly an indicator of an out-of-state driver. Not all states required front plates like Oregon.

She provided a detailed vehicle description when the sudden surge of the Jeep's engine coming even closer sent concern winding through her.

She hung up and turned to Darcie. "That Jeep behind us is gonna hit us if he doesn't back off."

Darcie raised her eyes to the rearview mirror. "Maybe that's his intent."

"You think it could be Marty?" Skyler's heart started racing. She searched the Jeep's windshield to get a look at the driver but couldn't see through the spitting rain.

"I'll change lanes to see if he follows." Darcie jerked into the other lane. Their rear end slid on the wet road before Darcie righted the vehicle.

The Jeep swung in behind them, closing the distance.

"He's going to ram us," Skyler cried out, wishing she was driving, as Darcie had never taken a defensive driving course.

Darcie pressed the gas pedal. They jetted forward, but the Jeep kept pace.

"Traffic's too heavy to try to lose him," Darcie said, her focus fixed ahead. "I can't go any faster."

The Jeep roared closer. Skyler braced for the impact she knew was coming. Her pulse throbbed in her head, the blood sounding like a rushing freight train.

His bumper rammed into them, shooting their car across the lane and toward the curb.

Darcie jerked the wheel hard and hit the brakes. Tires screeched against the road. The car slid, skidding wildly.

"Hang on! I can't stop." Panic carried Darcie's voice high.

The Jeep fell back. Sped up, roaring closer. He slammed

into them again. Metal twisted and groaned. Their car jumped the curb and Skyler was thrown forward. Her seat belt locked in place, cutting into her chest with an agonizing slice. Their car bumped the curb, and flew across the sidewalk, barely missing two pedestrians.

A massive pine loomed ahead in their path. *No, oh, no.* A lump of fear lodged in Skyler's throat.

Time seemed to slow.

Tick. Tick. Tick.

The tree grew larger. Seconds felt like minutes.

Skyler threw out her arm to protect Darcie from the jarring impact, then prayed for God to watch over them as they hurtled toward the enormous pine.

ELEVEN

Fairly vibrating with frustration from the hour spent with Paul Parsons, Logan pulled out of his parking space at the television station. He jerked off his tie, tossed it on the seat and snapped on his scanner for distraction. He'd given a full sixty minutes of valuable time to the interview and would need to hit the ground running when he reached the office.

He should be thinking about his to-do list, but Skyler's earlier comment about letting go to find peace kept nagging at him. If he'd had the presence of mind to respond rationally instead of letting her closeness muddle his thoughts, he'd have told her that her kind of peace was too hard to pin down. The kind of peace he was seeking could be had by making his father proud.

Simple. Measurable. Something Logan could obtain through hard work—had almost obtained. Would obtain if he stayed the course.

The scanner crackled, grabbing his attention. A harried dispatcher reported a single vehicle accident near the sheriff's office.

Skyler and Darcie?

Logan's heart squeezed.

"Relax," he told himself. "You were with Parsons long enough for Skyler to get home."

Or not.

She'd mentioned stopping to pick up a new cell. Phone companies were notoriously slow in finalizing transactions. He had to follow up or worry would distract him. He punched Jake's number on his screen.

"Seriously, you heard about the accident already?" Jake's irritation radiated through the phone.

"I heard there *was* an accident but not who was involved."

"Darcie and Skyler were run off the road. They crashed into a tree, but they're both okay. I'm on my way to pick them up now."

Logan exhaled in relief, but worry trailed behind. "Marty?"

"Looks like it."

Despite Jake's assurance that Skyler was fine, Logan had to see her to believe it. "I'm on my way. Should take me twenty minutes or so to get there." He ended the call before Jake could tell him to stay away.

He wound his car through traffic and soon caught sight of the crash scene. In a steep ditch, the bumper of Darcie's SUV had collapsed against a thick pine. Scanning the area for Skyler, he pulled to the side of the road.

When he spotted an ambulance and couldn't find her, his simmer of anxiety moved to a full-fledged boil. He bolted from the car and dug out his credentials, flashing them at a deputy protecting the scene. He rounded the ambulance and caught sight of Skyler sitting on the bumper, deep in conversation with Jake.

He'd expected to be concerned, but tightness in his chest and the inability to breathe surprised him.

Calm down. Now. Before you let her see how upset you are.

She'd wonder if he still cared and might think he planned to start something with her again. That would be the worst thing he could do to her.

Composed and professional. That's how he'd approach.

As he moved closer, he searched for any fresh injury. Her face was cherry red, likely from the air bag, and he could see she was barely holding back tears. A bruise was forming on her jaw, and she looked like she needed to be held. He longed to pull her into his arms and never let her out of his sight again. At least not until Marty was behind bars.

Jake shoved a pen into his pocket and flipped a small notepad closed while casting a quizzical look at Logan that said he obviously didn't have as tight of a control on his emotions as he'd thought.

He drew in a breath and buried his feelings as he'd done a million times with his father. Then he stepped up to Skyler with a renewed commitment to keep this professional.

"Any of the witnesses ID the driver as Marty?" he asked, pleased he'd managed a dispassionate tone.

Skyler's shoulders suddenly deflated, and she gave him a wary look.

Right. As he suspected. Her body language proved she didn't want him here, and he was right to keep things detached.

Jake pulled his shoulders back in a hard line as if protecting her. "All the witnesses can tell us is the driver was a white male with dark hair. Could be Marty. Or a million other guys."

"What about the vehicle?" Logan asked.

"The crash left red paint on Darcie's car." Jake scrubbed a hand over his face. "We'll collect it for analysis. If the Jeep still has the original paint job, the manufacturer can give us the model year and we can run a DMV search."

"Good," Logan said. "You put out an alert on the plates?"

Jake nodded. "No plates on the front or rear. Which might turn out to be a good thing. Even if the Jeep isn't pulled over from the vehicle description, the lack of plates should ensure a stop."

"*If* he stays on the road," Skyler added.

"Guess all we can do is wait then." With Skyler's near brush with death, Logan couldn't even raise an inkling of excitement over the possibility of this crash leading them to Marty.

Jake tucked his notepad away. "We were about to head back to the office to discuss this latest development. You're welcome to join us."

Skyler scowled at the news, but her frustration wouldn't deter Logan. She didn't know it yet, but he wasn't about to leave her protection to her squad for another minute. They could man the detail at her house, but if she stepped out her front door? He'd be right by her side until they put this crazy killer behind bars—no matter what he had to do to convince her.

While everyone took a seat in the conference room, Skyler tried to wrap her head around Logan's apparent lack of concern for her welfare at the accident scene. She wasn't surprised by his behavior. Not really, anyway. She'd expected him to put the investigation first. At least, logic said he would. Yet she'd thought he cared enough to ask if she was all right. Nope. Not once. He'd barely spared her a glance. Not even a single "how are you?"

And it hurt even worse than she'd expected.

The only hint that he was at all uneasy was his appearance when he'd arrived. Collar undone. Tie missing. Something must've really troubled him—though he'd hidden all signs of it by now. He'd buttoned up his shirt, put on his tie and looked in charge and in control. The consummate agent once again, standing at the end of the table ready to discuss the accident with the squad.

Cash dropped into the chair next to her and reclined. "Anyone ever think Marty might not be the one after Skyler?" His relaxed pose didn't fool Skyler. He was strung tighter than a guitar string. Though he loved adventure, he tried to control everything at work, and she could see he was feeling the same strain as she was.

"What do you mean?" Brady sat across from them. "Who else would do this?"

Cash clasped his hands behind his head. "From what you all tell me, Skyler's negotiated many cases where the outcome hasn't been favorable to the suspect. One of these suspects could be seeking revenge."

Jake perched on the end of the table. "She's received threats. We all have."

"So maybe it's time to start considering the people who've threatened her as potential suspects," Cash said.

Logan planted his hands on the table and fired a look at Cash. "Splitting our focus won't make it any easier to catch Marty."

"Thought you didn't want our help with that." Archer smirked.

Logan scowled at Archer. "You know what I meant. Don't try to distract us from the real point here."

"Ah, the point," Archer replied, his eyes never leaving Logan. "You want the focus to remain on Marty because you're hoping if he's after Skyler, you'll find him faster."

Logan seemed stunned as if Archer's comment might hold some truth. Frowning, he shook his head and made eye contact with each team member, ending with her. "I wouldn't put you in danger even if it meant Marty was served to me on a silver platter. If you think it's worth a look at prior negotiations, then I suggest you do it and do it now."

Skyler couldn't stop the warm feeling Logan's comment brought. And it wasn't just empty words—she could tell. She watched the rise and fall of his chest as he wrestled to calm his emotions.

Actions speak louder than words, she'd said to him in the car that morning. His actions were telling her he cared. He may not have asked about her at the accident scene and may not have been able to make a commitment to her, but he did care.

"Reviewing the cases sounds like a good idea to me," Darcie said, bringing Skyler back.

She nodded her agreement. "In fact, if Jake will let me stay for a few hours, I'll start on them right now."

Jake frowned. "Need I remind you that you're on medical leave? And the accident didn't improve anything."

She resisted crossing her arms and taking a stand that would make him dig his heels in deeper. "Sitting here looking at the files is nearly the same as sitting in front of my computer at home."

"You shouldn't be in front of your computer. You should be resting your eyes and that stubborn brain of yours." He lifted his hand as if he planned to thump her head, then let it drop.

"How about a compromise?" she suggested. "I'll review files for a few hours, then go home and rest."

Shaking his head, Jake groaned. "I'll give you two hours just to get you off my case. Two hours, Skyler. That's all. In the back conference room where no one will see you or I'll catch heat for letting you stay. Got it?"

"Got it." She smiled sincerely.

Logan took a step closer to the table. "Since the schedule for your protection detail isn't finished yet, I'll hang around to give you a ride home." He paused and made eye contact with her as if he expected her to argue. "I'll also stay with you until someone else can arrange to take over."

"I really appreciate your freeing me up, Logan," Jake said before Skyler could comment. "I'd rather not get behind today if it can be helped." He got to his feet, signaling the end of their discussion, but Jake's change from calling Logan Suit to using his real name lingered in Skyler's mind.

Was Logan earning Jake's trust? Or was she simply hoping for that so she didn't feel bad about how she was letting him get to her?

He crossed the room, his phone in hand. "I just got a text from my office. They found a receipt in Nicole's pocket for a local makeup store, and Wagner is emailing a picture of it to me. Once I receive it, I'll head over to talk with the shop owner while you're still safe here."

Did he really think she'd stay at the office to search files for a long shot when they had a sure lead? "Since this is about makeup, wouldn't a woman's perspective be helpful? I'd like to come with you."

Something unreadable shimmered in his eyes, but he didn't speak.

She expected him to refuse her request, so she rushed on. "If you're worried about another attack from Marty or whoever ran us off the road, it's unlikely he'll try anything again so soon."

"I'm not worried about that." He took a step closer, his gaze warm and personal. "You keep claiming you're fine, but I'm concerned you're hiding pain to keep working. You may not believe me, but I really do want what's best for you, Skyler. If that means staying here, then that's what I want."

She *did* believe him. A smile slipped out before she clamped down on her lips and forced her mind onto the job. "I'm fine. Can I come with you?"

He peered at her closely. She worked hard not to squirm under his scrutiny and waited him out.

"You can come along." He dug his car keys out of his pocket. "First, I need to grab my computer from the car to print a few things. Is there anything I can get for you while I'm out? Maybe a cup of green tea."

"No, thanks," she said. She watched him walk away, feeling surprised but pleased that he remembered the kind of tea she loved.

Frowning, Darcie got up and crossed over to Skyler. She

was thankful color had returned to Darcie's face after the accident. She made several trips back to her native Florida each year, and she never had that pasty-white complexion of most Portlanders. But when the car crashed...

The thought of almost losing her best friend made Skyler feel ill. She grabbed her in a hug, not caring about the deep bruise from her seat belt.

"I'm so glad you didn't get hurt in the crash," Skyler whispered.

Darcie returned the hug, then pushed back and appraised Skyler. She thought to turn away, but she knew that would make Darcie search even harder.

"What?" Skyler asked after Darcie remained mute for long uncomfortable moments.

Darcie stepped back. "That look in your eyes has me worried. You're obviously more than attracted to Logan."

"Don't worry so much." Skyler made sure to bury any longing for Logan she felt deep inside, where it couldn't surface again.

"I can't help it. You're giving me reason to worry."

"No need. I know how to protect my heart." Skyler hoped if she kept saying the words that she'd soon start to believe they were true.

Logan held the door for Skyler to enter the theatrical makeup store. Catering to local movie production companies, Logan expected a more polished interior, but it wasn't much more than a hole in the wall. Floor-to-ceiling shelves holding brightly colored containers filled two walls. An antique barber's chair sat at the back near a lighted mirror and table littered with cosmetic samples.

A woman dressed in a vibrant rainbow of colors with a large snake tattoo circling her neck stood behind a counter pricing tubes of makeup. She eyed Logan skeptically. "Can I help you?"

Wagner had said the owner was expecting them, but this woman seemed more like a salesperson than his idea of a shop owner. "I'm looking for Olivia Stone."

Her eyes narrowed. "I'm Olivia."

Logan held up his ID. "Logan Hunter, FBI. This is my associate Skyler Brennan."

"Right. You're looking for a woman who bought makeup here."

Logan pulled the printed photo of the receipt from his suit pocket. "She paid cash, so we know you won't have any financial information, but we hoped you might have surveillance footage for the time of her purchase."

"Sorry. No cameras." Olivia peered at the receipt. "I remember her, though. She asked for the best tattoo concealer I had. Guess she thought I might occasionally need to cover this bad boy up." Olivia ran her fingers over the coiling snake.

"Did she have a tattoo?" Logan asked.

Olivia nodded, making the snake appear to open and close its mouth. "One that I could see. On her forearm. Two closed fists with Rose City inked on the knuckles. She said it was the logo for the Rose City Rollers."

"Women's Roller Derby?" Skyler's voice rose in surprise.

"Yeah. She said she was a founding member back in '04."

Skyler shot Logan an excited look before focusing on Olivia again. "How can you be sure you're remembering the right woman?"

"Simple. I only had three concealer compacts in stock. She purchased all three of them. So until I get my next shipment, no one else could've bought one."

"Sounds like the woman we're looking for," Logan said. "Was she alone that day?"

"Nah, she had a guy with her."

"Tell me about them."

Olivia set the receipt on the counter and settled on a tall

wooden stool. "He was kinda flighty, like he might be high or something, but she was nice as could be. She said she was a professional makeup artist, and I believed her."

"Why?" Skyler asked.

"We had a good long talk about products. She knew her stuff."

Logan pulled out a picture printed from bank surveillance footage. "Could this be the same couple?"

Olivia studied the photo. "Maybe. They're both the right size and their hair color is the same, but their facial features are different. The woman's nose in the picture is much broader and more pronounced. Plus her cheeks are higher, as are his. And the guy who came in here had scarring from acne, which isn't in the picture."

"Based on your perception of her abilities as a makeup artist, could they have changed their appearance in this manner with the products they purchased?" Logan tapped the receipt.

She lifted the picture closer. "The concealer she bought could make the guy's skin look like this, and she could've used the wax to alter their cheeks and noses."

"So yes?" Logan clarified.

"Yes." She stared at Logan, her eyes awash with concern. "Did they rob a bank or something?"

"I'm not at liberty to discuss that." Logan took the picture back and picked up the receipt. "If I arranged for you to meet with a sketch artist, do you think you could describe them as they looked the day they came in here?"

"Her for sure. The guy?" She shrugged. "I can try, but he never stood still, so I didn't get a real good look at him."

Logan needed a sketch of Marty, not Nicole, but he'd still proceed in the event Olivia remembered more than she thought. "Would you mind waiting for a moment while I schedule a sketch artist?"

"No problem."

Logan stepped to the side to call his office. As he waited, he heard Skyler ask Olivia about Marty wearing a ring. Olivia replied that she hadn't noticed one. When Logan had the session arranged for tomorrow at ten, he joined them again and confirmed Olivia's availability.

"You've been most helpful, Ms. Stone." He pulled out his business card and jotted his cell number on the back. "Please call if you think of anything else."

She nodded seriously. "Oh, hey, you should check out the Oregon Media Production Association's website. It's a nonprofit organization for commercial, film and TV professionals. And try the Portland Area Theatre Alliance, too. They might know this woman."

Logan made note of the organizations' names, then escorted Skyler to the car. The moment she sat, she started rubbing her temples.

He watched her for a moment and didn't like how washed-out she appeared. "Headache getting worse?"

"Yeah."

"The adrenaline from the crash is probably subsiding." She didn't seem to buck under his attention, which was a red flag.

"Do you want me to take you home instead of the office?" he asked gently, though he wanted to fire up the car and force her to go home.

"I'd like to say I could do some research on my files, but I know when I've reached my limit." She looked so sad.

His heart constricted from the suffering she was going through. He longed to hold her. To make her pain go away. *So what if he did?*

It was no use thinking about what he longed to do when she'd made it perfectly clear that his touch would only make things worse.

TWELVE

Skyler woke after a long nap to the smell of pungent garlic snaking under her door. Surprisingly, she was no longer nauseous and hunger pangs pinched her stomach. The headache had decreased to a dull throb, something she could easily manage with a few aspirin. Still she rose slowly to check for vertigo.

No spinning or wooziness. Maybe she was on the mend. She freshened up, changing her rumpled shirt and jeans for comfy yoga pants and a T-shirt. She ran a comb through her hair and put on lightly tinted lip gloss.

Not because Logan's here, she told herself. Though he'd promised to stay at the firehouse to make calls while she napped, one of the team members had likely come home to cook by now and had sent Logan packing. Certainly Logan wouldn't be cooking. He'd never even boiled water as far as she knew.

Now ravenous, she hurried down the hall, hoping someone took pity on them and kept Cash from cooking. At the kitchen door, her steps faltered.

Logan stood at the stove, stirring a small pot. He'd removed his jacket and tie and rolled the cuffs of his white shirt, revealing strong, masculine arms. Steam rose from a larger pot and disappeared into the air around his head.

Logan made dinner. Correction: Logan made dinner for *her.*

Her mouth fell open. He was inches from his promotion and should be working his case, yet he'd taken the time to make dinner for her. He was obviously trying to mend the rift between them.

He looked up and smiled. "Are you feeling better?" His voice was low and warm.

"You cooked." She regretted how dumb she sounded, but that was all she could come up with when her heart was doing a silly clip-clop over the homey scene and the warmth of his smile.

He chuckled. "Crazy, right? I made spaghetti. Turns out it's not that hard." He tapped his laptop sitting on the island. "At least not with instructions from the internet."

She wanted to laugh over his need for directions on how to boil noodles and heat up jarred sauce, but it would hurt his feelings. "You didn't need to do this."

"I know, but I thought if you woke up hungry, I'd have something ready for you."

"I'm starving, and I really do appreciate it." He preened at her gratitude, making her melt.

Don't read too much into this, she cautioned herself.

"Let me grab the salad and garlic bread so we can eat." He turned to the oven and pulled out a prepackaged loaf of bread.

He sliced the bread and tossed the salad, then turned to her. "Let's eat in here instead of hauling everything into the dining room. How about moving my computer so I can lay out the plates?"

She reached for his laptop and the screen came to life, revealing a page filled with colorful class rings. *Poof,* her warm feelings vanished. "You got the pictures of the rings."

"Yeah, I just got the email." He set plates on the island. "I was hoping you'd look at them before I took off tonight."

"I can do it now."

"And let your dinner get cold?" He mocked offense and closed his computer. "Not after I slaved over a hot stove all afternoon you won't."

She couldn't hide her surprise, but, thankfully, he turned away before seeing it and asking questions. She set his computer at the end of the island.

He laid two place settings, then piled noodles and sauce on her plate and added a crispy slice of garlic bread. He loaded a bowl with salad and slid it across the island. "Dig in."

She twirled a bite onto her fork and savored the rich sauce. "Not bad. In fact, pretty good."

He settled down behind his plate. "It's nothing and you know it."

"Honestly, it *is* something. Cash was going to cook to make up for last night. He would've overcooked the noodles and burned the sauce. And don't get me started on what he would've done to the bread. We often choose to eat out on his night so he doesn't attempt to cook."

"I can sympathize with him. This dinner could've gone wrong for me." He tucked into his food.

She set down her fork and picked up the bread. "Is this a skill you learned in Chicago?"

"Nah. You know me. I'm hardly home and get all my meals from takeout. Plus it's not worth the effort when you eat alone."

"So you're not dating then?"

His head shot up. "Way to come right out and ask."

"And way to not answer."

"I'm not dating."

Her heart soared again, but she immediately tamped it down. "No eligible women in Chicago?"

"I had no desire to look. Not after…" His voice fell off and his eyes connected with hers for a brief moment before he looked down at his plate. "The job keeps me busy. Real busy."

"Tell me about the work," she said sincerely, though she didn't like hearing him confirm that his job was still number one in his life.

He took a drink of water, then shared details of his investigations and his coworkers. His voice and face were animated and it was obvious how much he thrived on his work.

"And your parents?" she asked. "How are they?"

He shrugged. "The same. Busy. Driven."

Just like you.

"I guess you haven't taken the time to explore the city."

"No. When you're alone…" His stared over her head, and she caught a hint of sadness in his eyes. "The job's good, though."

She believed he should take pride and joy in his work—after all, her job was important to her, too—but she also had friendships with her teammates and she found fulfillment through her charity.

What about what you don't have? Love. The thought spiraled out of nowhere, catching her by surprise.

She hated to admit it, but her life paralleled his in the relationship department. She'd turned inward to avoid being hurt again and had cut herself off from experiences to avoid additional heartache. Now she couldn't help but wonder what her defensive posture had caused her to miss out on.

Had she been kidding herself all this time saying she was fine on her own? Did she really want a man to share her life with? A man to sit down to a cozy dinner with? To have children with and shower them with the love she'd never had?

Even if the answer was yes, she wasn't ready to open herself up and risk the pain again. Being alone right now was the best course for her life.

Alone didn't break hearts and leave deep wounds. Alone didn't bring pain. Alone, she did just fine.

"Earth to Skyler," he said, searching her eyes. "Where'd you go all of a sudden?"

"Just thinking."

"Are you worried about Marty?"

"Marty?" she asked, having totally forgotten about the investigation.

"You know, the guy who wants to kill you?" He sounded upset that she wasn't taking the threat seriously.

It served as the reminder she needed to keep her emotions in check. "Were there any new developments in the case while I was sleeping? Other than the rings, I mean."

"Not exactly. Wagner met with the Rose City Rollers. They didn't recognize Nicole's picture, but none of the current staff worked there in 2004. They do have old team rosters in off-site storage. It'll take time to get them. They suggested we check out their website forums to ask if anyone remembers the '04 players. My team has started working on that while I called the people from the associations Olivia gave us."

"Any success?"

"Not yet, but I'm hopeful."

"So at the moment, we're left with the college rings as our only workable lead." She pulled the computer closer. "I'd like to look at them while I finish eating."

"Let me open the file for you," he said and came to stand behind her. He leaned even closer to use the track pad. She jerked back from him, garnering a raise of his eyebrows.

"Here you go." The pictures blinked onto the screen. He returned to his stool and attacked his salad with a vengeance. Maybe he was experiencing the same frustrating emotions she was feeling.

So what? Nothing had changed.

She turned her attention to his computer and scrolled down, page after page until she reached the bottom without seeing Marty's ring. She fought back her disappointment. "Sorry, it's not here."

"You're sure?"

"Yes." She closed the computer.

"Then I'll have the team widen the geographic search and prepare a new list."

"Good."

They finished eating in silence. Forks clanking on plates and salad bowls the only sound. The air was rife with tension. The moment she finished eating, she hopped to her feet and started gathering plates.

He joined her and opened the dishwasher. Though he didn't cook, he'd always helped clean up. "By the way, Jake called. He said the squad was on a callout and wouldn't be home until after dinner."

She met his gaze. "You can go if you need to."

"That's not why I mentioned it."

"Then why?"

"Honestly?" he asked, his gaze lingering on hers. "I hoped small talk would ease this tension that keeps popping up between us."

"Doesn't seem to be working, does it?"

He shook his head.

"I really am okay on my own," she said. "In fact, since I napped so long, I probably won't sleep tonight, and that means it's a perfect time to buy party supplies that the robbery interrupted."

He planted a hand on the counter. "I'd rather you didn't go out at all. And if you do, you certainly can't go alone."

"I really don't have a choice. The party's this weekend and I won't disappoint these families."

"I knew you'd say that, but I had to try." He gave her the barest of smiles. "At least let me drive you."

Being in a confined car with him was the last thing she

needed. "You must have other things to do for the investigation."

He shrugged and turned back to the dishwasher. "I always enjoyed helping with the parties. It would be fun to do it again."

"So that wasn't a lie?" The words shot out before she thought to censor them.

"What?" His head jerked up.

She saw no reason to sugarcoat her reply. "So many of the things we did together—going to church, helping the shelter—don't seem to be part of your life anymore, so I thought maybe they didn't mean as much to you as I once believed. Maybe you worked with the charity because I wanted you to, not because you enjoyed it."

"Helping the families gave meaning to my life and I did it solely to help them." He swallowed hard as if the words stuck in his throat.

"I didn't mean to offend you."

"Well, you did." His eyes dark and furious, he closed the dishwasher hard and started unrolling his sleeves. "Now that you know where I stand, let's get those supplies."

Skyler grabbed her purse, and Logan shrugged into his suit jacket. He went outside first. "Stay here until I clear the area."

Hand on his weapon, he made a lingering sweep of the property, then motioned for her to join him. The moment she stepped outside, a fine mist dampened her hair. During her nap, it had turned even colder, and the rain intensified the chill. She didn't doubt the snow predicted for later in the week would actually occur. They hurried toward his car, the tension palpable between them.

He merged into traffic but kept his mouth clamped tight. *Fine. Don't talk to me.*

She'd pretty much struck out or offended him with everything she'd said tonight, so she was glad for the silence.

Or not. At least she couldn't seem to quit looking at him to see if he was still mad.

Jaw firm, his gaze kept going to the rearview mirror, reminding her that she should be more concerned with the potential danger to her life than with Logan's mood or how she felt about him.

She looked in the side mirror, and her heart sank. "Is that a red Jeep behind us?"

"Yes," he answered, not taking his eyes from the mirror.

"Coincidence?"

"I don't believe in them. Plus the car doesn't have a front plate. It's too dark to see if there's front end damage."

Skyler looked in the mirror again. Large water droplets ran down the glass, blurring her view. She searched over her shoulder through the water spitting from their tires. She couldn't get a clear view of the front end. She did confirm the lighted spot where a license plate should be was empty.

They continued on, but the Jeep remained at a distance until they hit the main road. Then it came gunning for them.

Memories of the accident with Darcie rushed back. "This feels like this morning. He's gonna ram us."

"Probably," Logan said, his voice deadly calm. "At least he plans to try."

"Can't you evade him?"

He looked in the mirror again. "Not if I want to arrest him, no."

Right. Arrest him and get the promotion. The reason for Logan's existence. "You're really considering letting him ram us so you can get that job?"

He gave her a confused look. "Call nine-one-one and hold on."

She made the call, then prepared herself for the wild ride that she knew was coming.

THIRTEEN

Unbelievable. Skyler really thought Logan would let the Jeep plow into them just so he could catch Marty. He'd simply wanted to make sure she understood evading Marty meant he'd get away—and probably come after her again.

He searched ahead for an escape and spotted an alley on the left. He quickly changed lanes. The car slid wildly on the wet pavement for a moment. He saw Skyler put her hand on the dash to brace herself for another impact. Wouldn't happen. Not if he had anything to say about it.

"Hold on tighter," he warned. "We're turning left into an alley ahead."

"At this speed? In front of all this traffic?" Anxiety lifted her voice higher.

"I can do it. You could, too. We're both trained for this very thing, but Marty isn't. He'll never make the turn." Logan squeezed her hand. "You trust me?"

"I trust you to keep me safe."

He heard the hesitation in her tone, and didn't like the implication that she didn't trust him in any other area of life. He let go of her hand and gripped the wheel. "Here we go."

He cranked the wheel hard.

The car responded with a lurch that unsettled him for a moment. The tires squealed across the pavement. The rear

end fishtailed wildly before he wrestled the car into sub-
mission.

Horns blared into the night. Cars screeched to a stop,
but they needn't have. He'd timed it perfectly and they were
sailing down an alley while the Jeep continued down the
main road.

Blowing out a breath, Logan made a few more turns,
leaving no trail for Marty to follow. He slowed and pulled
to the curb. He looked at Skyler to make sure she was okay.
She was shaken but holding her own. No tears or hysterics.
She really was a strong woman.

"I didn't think you'd let Marty go like that. Thank you."
She let out a long breath and dragged in another. "I'm not
sure I could've handled another crash."

Her words creased his heart. Her statement meant as a
thank-you made him sound pathetic.

Had he really sunk so low in her eyes that she thought
he'd risk anyone's life—particularly hers—to advance his
career?

If she did, maybe it was high time he took a long look in
the mirror to figure out what she was seeing. Then he could
decide if there was still time to change it before he actually
turned into the pathetic guy she seemed to believe him to be.

"Now, what have I forgotten to get?" Skyler stared at the
shelf in the party supply store.

Logan gestured at the cart chock-full of party supplies.
"With all this stuff, you can't possibly have forgotten a
thing. Of course, if you'd made a list…"

She fired a testy look at him. Since Marty wouldn't likely
come after her again tonight, they'd agreed to forget all
about the near crash and keep things light as they shopped.
But bringing up an area they'd argued about in the past
wasn't keeping things light in her book. "You're not seriously going there, are you?"

His lips curled in a cute grin, instantly melting her anger. It had been so long since he'd teased her, she hadn't recognized it at first. Or maybe she didn't want to recognize it and let down her guard.

She ignored the warning bells clanging in her head and playfully swatted a hand at him. "Oh, it's that way, is it? Well, Mr. Buttoned-Down Suit, who needs a list and has to plan for every minute of the day, it wouldn't hurt you to go with the flow every now and then."

He grabbed her hand and held fast. "Maybe you're right, but the opposite is true for you, too."

His touch made her remember the way they'd usually cuddled to make up after their differences caused them to argue. Making up was almost worth the fights.

"I really did love working on these events with you. We were a good team, weren't we?" He let go of her hand.

"You mean despite the fact that we're extreme opposites," she said lightly, though she took his comment very seriously.

His gaze dug deep into her eyes. "But we were well matched, too. You were such a calming influence on me."

Despite her desire to stay detached, she had to agree with him. By putting them together, God made them each so much stronger. More balanced and whole. A thought that sent panic racing through her veins.

He moved closer, his eyes still riveted on hers. Was he going to lean down and kiss her? Did she want him to? Her breath caught in her throat in anticipation.

This was wrong—so wrong—and would end in more pain when he remembered his priorities, but in this moment, she couldn't bring herself to stop.

A loud crash boomed from the aisle next to them. He lurched back. His hand went for his weapon, his eyes alert and aware.

"Relax." She drew in a cleansing breath. "Sounded like someone knocked into a display."

"I'm not taking any chances. Stay here." He crept to the end of the aisle, then disappeared around the corner.

She doubted Marty was in the store, but the incident gave her time to pull her head out of the clouds.

By the time he returned, her feet were firmly on the ground again, where she intended to keep them. No matter the temptation he provided.

"You were right. It was a display." His gaze still held a measure of interest for her.

"We should get going." She quickly turned away though it was the last thing she really wanted to do.

"Skyler?" He stepped in front of her.

She ignored him and started pushing the cart toward the checkout. "If I've forgotten something, I'll come back."

"See, that's where a list would've helped." He huffed a quick laugh, but she didn't find any humor in their verbal sparring anymore.

"What fun is there in that?" she said. "If I have to come back, I could find something else that will make the party even more special. Or find something on sale or run into someone I haven't seen in ages. Life's an adventure. Live it like one."

"I prefer to think life's a marathon. Train for it, set your sights on the finish line and succeed."

"Let's agree to disagree, shall we, before we get into an argument for real."

"Okay," he said, sounding confused by her about-face.

She helped him unload the cart, then paid for the party supplies. Under his watchful eye, they loaded the car and headed home. Though neither spoke, he kept glancing at her. He was probably trying to figure out why she'd clammed up, but there was no point in talking about this thing between them. It was going nowhere so why bother?

They dragged her stash into the family room, and found the squad grouped around the TV watching the news.

"Good." Jake looked up from his large leather recliner. "The anchors have been teasing us about an upcoming story on the robbery. I was hoping you'd get home in time to see it."

She took a seat next to Darcie on the sofa. Logan perched on the arm beside her when she hoped he'd sit elsewhere.

Each of her teammates checked her out in their own way. Cash, a direct, sharp stare. Brady, a quick glance before moving on to something else. Archer, from under eyelids that seemed to be closing. And Darcie, a squeeze of Skyler's knee. They had different methods, but Skyler always felt loved around them.

"So." Brady's Minnesota accent drew the word out as he gestured at the TV. "Here we go."

The story started out in a studio where Paul Parsons interviewed Logan. Skyler actually enjoyed the interview. Not only because Logan was well-spoken, handling or adeptly sidestepping Parsons's questions, but because she could really study him without fearing he'd catch her in the act.

"Good job, man," Jake said when the interview ended. "I know how hard those things can be."

"Shh." Darcie put a finger to her lips. "The story's not over."

The screen flashed to Parsons in front of a video feed for the Salem robbery. "We discovered an interesting development today. Take a look at the footage from a prior robbery."

"How'd they get access to the video?" Archer asked.

"We gave the local press a snippet hoping they'd play it and someone would recognize the robbers," Logan replied.

"Keep a good eye on the video," Parsons said. "As you can see, Clyde is wearing a military-issue ammo bag on his belt. We've begun an in-depth investigation into the possibility that Clyde is former military." Parsons raised an eyebrow and looked pointedly into the camera. "We can only hope the FBI is planning to do the same thing."

Logan groaned.

"That Parsons is such a doofus." Brady stretched, the sleeves of his flannel shirt staining from the effort. "If he'd taken half a second to investigate before this segment, he'd have figured out you can buy an ammo bag at any surplus store or even on eBay."

"Have you spoken to the FBI about this lead?" the female anchor, a brunette in a severe black suit, asked Parsons.

"I've tried, but after my interview with Agent Hunter, he hasn't returned my calls."

Logan scowled. "He makes it sound like I've avoided him when he only texted me once this afternoon."

"In an earlier story," the anchor continued, "you mentioned a red Jeep in connection to the case, along with a threat to Deputy Brennan's life. Might this be related to the military lead somehow?"

"Seems to me it's all related, and our viewers can be assured that I won't rest until I figure out the connection."

"There you have it, folks. Excellent reporting by our own Paul Parsons, as usual," the anchor said. "Let's hope the FBI is being equally diligent."

Jake stabbed his thumb into the remote control, and the TV went dark. "I get so tired of the media second-guessing police work. It's like they don't think we know how to run an investigation. You're doing everything you're supposed to and jumping to attention every time some loudmouth reporter snaps his fingers won't get the job done any better or faster."

"Tell that to my supervisor." Logan blew out a frustrated breath. "He'll be all over me for not getting back to Parsons the second he texted."

Instead, you spent time with me, Skyler thought.

"Since you didn't mention this lead," Jake said, "I'm guessing you've already ruled it out."

Logan nodded. "After seeing the ammo bag in the Salem

robbery, we started searching military databases. We looked for males from L.A. and the surrounding area who fit the right age and physical profile. No viable matches yet. And, of course, the recent search for Nicole's prints told us she didn't serve in the military."

Something about the military connection bothered Skyler, but she couldn't seem to figure out what it was, so she sat back, pondering.

Cash casually crossed his worn cowboy boots, looking relaxed, until he aimed one of his piercing looks at Logan. "Since you haven't been able to confirm Marty's from L.A. or even the West Coast for that matter, your limited database searches don't rule out a military connection."

Logan met Cash's gaze with a confident one of his own. He didn't seem as upset with the squad's questions as he had been yesterday. Was he starting to feel more comfortable around them—and vice versa? Jake, at least, seemed to be showing Logan more acceptance.

"We've planned for that," Logan said. "Each time a search fails to pan out, the team increases the search radius. Now that we have a first name, we've ruled out all Martins and Martys in the western U.S. We'll search the entire country if we have to, but it'll take a couple of days to get it done."

"A few more days with Skyler in danger." Darcie started chewing on her thumbnail.

Jake looked at Darcie. "*If* Marty's even the one after her."

"What?" Skyler couldn't control her surprise. "You don't think it's Marty anymore, either?"

Jake shrugged. "I'm just keeping my options open."

Logan scowled at Jake. "My gut still says Marty's our guy, and we need to keep our focus on him."

Jake sat up straighter. "I believe in trusting gut feelings in an investigation, but *my* gut is saying it might not be Marty. So where does that leave us?"

"With two guys whose guts are hurting," Darcie said, her expression deadpan.

The squad erupted in laughter. Despite Logan's frustration with this investigation, Skyler was pleased to see him join in. She hadn't seen him laugh or even smile much since he'd come back, and his joy made her happy. Unreasonably happy.

"Good one, Darcie." Cash dropped his boot to the floor and leaned forward to bump fists with her. "Glad to see the real you for a change. You've been far too crabby the past few days."

She held a hand to her chest in mock offense. "*Moi?* Crabby?"

"If the shoe fits." Archer grinned.

"Yeah, what he said," Brady tacked on.

Darcie held up her hands. "Okay, okay, I get it. Since you *ladies* are so sensitive, I'll try to be more cheerful."

Laughter spilled through the room again. Instead of smiling along this time, sadness crowded out the joy on Logan's face, making Skyler wonder about his thoughts.

"In all seriousness," Jake said, reining them in, "I recommend Skyler gets started on those old case files while Logan focuses on Marty."

"I agree," Archer added. "It'll keep her busy and stuck at home or in the office wh—"

"Gee, thanks," Skyler interrupted.

"Let me finish," Archer said. "I was going to add where you'll be out of danger and hopefully you'll find another viable suspect."

"That's better, then." She grinned at him. "With Jake's permission, I'll work on the files at the office in the morning."

Jake met her gaze. "Same criteria. Two hours. That's it."

Logan looked down on her. His tight expression told her she wouldn't like what he was about to say. "With the monster of a headache you had today, do you think reviewing files is such a good idea?"

Darcie shifted on the sofa. "You had a bad headache again?"

"Earlier, but it's okay now," she said as she avoided Darcie's gaze.

"Look at me," Darcie demanded.

Skyler turned and wasn't surprised to see the concern in Darcie's eyes.

"I'm fine, Mom." Skyler laughed to lighten her friend's mood, but it didn't change her expression.

Darcie crossed her arms. "I'm not so sure about that."

"Maybe a follow-up with the doctor is in order," Jake suggested.

"Wouldn't hurt to get things checked out, squirt," Cash weighed in.

Logan opened his mouth to speak, but she wasn't about to let him. She stood. "You can all stop worrying about me, okay? I may be on medical leave, but it's just a precaution. I promise to heed any warning signs and rest when needed, just like I did today. But there's no way I'm sitting on the sidelines for this investigation unless it's absolutely necessary."

Logan raked his gaze over her, his frustration evident.

"End of discussion," Skyler said. She looked around the room until she was certain there would be no further talk of her sitting this out.

This was her life they were talking about, and it was only right that she be allowed to take an active part in finding the person who was doing his very best to end it.

FOURTEEN

In the small conference room, Skyler closed another case file and sat back to take a few deep breaths. Her head had been throbbing all morning. Aspirin barely touched the pain. Plus her eyes were glazing over from looking at tons and tons of paperwork. But powering through the pain had paid off. She'd separated out a nice stack of former hostage cases to follow up on.

She rubbed fingers into her temples and closed her eyes, putting all her concentration into relaxing. She wished she could do a few yoga stretches, but the headache left her so dizzy, she'd likely fall to the floor.

"Headache worse?" Logan's voice came from right beside her.

Her head shot up. "Do you always sneak up on people like that? You scared me."

"I didn't sneak. You were too wrapped up in trying to tame that headache." He sat on the edge of the table. "Is it as bad as yesterday?"

She didn't want to admit it, but her headache bordered on the same intensity. She wouldn't lie, so she shrugged.

"C'mon." He tugged her to her feet. "We're going to the E.R. to see Dr. Baker."

She planted her feet and eyed him. "I don't remember telling you the name of the doctor who treated me."

"You didn't. I did a little digging and called him yesterday while you were napping. He said if the headache didn't improve, you should come back."

The urge to argue was strong, but it was countered by joy over him caring enough to call the doctor when he had so much else to do. And that hesitation made her madder. Not at him, but at herself for being such a fool when it came to him.

"How many times do I have to tell you, I don't need you taking over my life?" she demanded, taking her frustration out on him. She hated how bitter and mean she sounded, but even when she hit the mark, making him cringe, she didn't apologize. Any rift between them was a good way of keeping her feelings in check.

"I was only doing what I thought was best for you." His voice was soft and tender, making her feel even worse. "What's so bad about seeing the doctor?"

"He could extend my leave."

"Then it needs to be extended. I know you want to help with the case, but maybe the headache is God's way of telling you to stay put." He took her hand.

"Now you want to consider God's plan? When it's *convenient?*" She let her words fly without thinking and jerked free.

He recoiled as if he'd been bitten by a viper. Which was exactly what she was acting like. She'd taken the strain of the past few days out on him when he didn't deserve it.

"I'm sorry." She met his gaze and tried to transmit her sincerity. "That was uncalled for."

He shoved his hands into his pockets but didn't look away. "It's okay. You're right. I haven't been living my life by my faith. It's hypocritical of me to involve God now. But don't let anything I say or do stand in the way of letting the doctor check you out. Please."

It was the softly uttered *please* tagged on the end, the

warmth in his tone when all she deserved was his anger, that got to her.

"Fine," she said and marched toward the door. Quickly, before she really started to believe that he cared enough about her to do something about it.

The pain—that heartrending pain another person could cause with simple words—had taken Logan by surprise. As he walked down the hallway behind Skyler, he could hardly breathe for the tightness in his gut. He'd felt like this hundreds—maybe thousands—of times with his father. But the only time Skyler had left him reeling was the day he'd told her he was leaving and she'd let her hurt and rage fly.

His heart had ached that day and it was hurting now. Not from her comment about his faith. That he deserved. Not even from the finality in her tone when she'd said she didn't need him in her life. No, the pain came from the way she said it. The coldness in her gaze. He felt in his bones how badly he'd hurt her. He doubted he'd ever be able to make up for it, and desperately wanted to make things right between them.

"Skyler, stop!" He charged after her as she pushed open the exit door. He grabbed her arm, stopping her from heading outside.

"Don't run like that again," he warned, his pulse beating double time. "You've had two attempts on your life, and Marty could be out there waiting for you."

"I'm sorry. I wasn't thinking." She blew out a breath, lifting her bangs. "I won't do it again."

He was thrown off guard by her easy acquiescence and couldn't think of what to say next.

"What were you thinking, Skyler?" Cash's raised voice came from behind them.

Logan turned to find the muscle-bound guy striding down the hallway, his face red with anger. He was fierce and dangerous-looking, and Logan could easily imagine him as a soldier battling enemies of the country.

Skyler took a step back. "I wasn't thinking."

"Well, start," Cash barked at her. "We have protocols in place for a reason, and we need to follow them all the time. Not just when we feel like it."

Skyler seemed near tears, but Cash didn't back down. His anger seemed out of proportion for the situation, making Logan wonder what was going through the guy's mind. Logan didn't ask, though. It wasn't really any of his business. And besides, Cash had definitely gotten Skyler's attention. In the long run, the warning would serve her well.

"We'll clear the parking lot before you take another step," Cash added.

She bit her trembling lip and stood back. Logan almost stopped to give her a hug, but after their conversation just now, he knew that was the last thing she'd want, so he headed outside after Cash.

Without saying a word, Cash went left and Logan right. They carefully searched the parking lot, then, with a nod of agreement, they returned to Skyler.

"We're clear, but stick close to him, all right?" Cash said to Skyler, his voice softer now.

She nodded, the crushed look still on her face.

Logan took her arm and was grateful when she didn't cringe. He exited the rear of the building, keeping her close by his side. They were halfway to the car when a flash in the far trees caught his attention.

"Sniper!" He jerked Skyler to him and tumbled to the ground.

A gunshot pierced the air.

Logan took the brunt of the fall on his shoulder and rolled them behind a squad car as the bullet whizzed overhead. The rough gravel bit through his shirt, but he held fast.

"You okay?" he asked as he drew his weapon and came to his feet.

"Yes." Her voice was small, but her answer came without hesitation.

He risked a quick look at her and caught sight of her face pale with shock. He couldn't do anything about it. Not now. Now his focus needed to be on the shooter. He squatted behind the side panel. Skyler drew her own gun and slowly moved to a sitting position. He put a hand on her shoulder to keep her from rising into the line of fire.

He quickly appraised her and didn't like the lack of focus he found. "Are you really okay?"

"Yes." Her eyes were wide, her chin trembling. Though she was a strong police officer, she'd nearly lost her life again, and she wasn't thinking clearly.

"They'll have heard the shot inside," he said, turning back to the shooter. "We'll sit tight until reinforcements come pouring out the door." Adrenaline coursed through his veins, but he wouldn't let it distract him. Breathing slow and deep to steady his nerves, he kept his focus trained on the trees.

The door creaked open.

"Skyler?" Cash's voice rang out from behind the cracked door.

"She's fine," Logan yelled. "I saw the muzzle flash. A single shot from the woods across the lot. About fifty feet in from the road. If the guy's smart, he'll know you'll be swarming in on him and he's bolted, but we'll hunker down here until you give us the all clear."

"We'll get into our tactical gear and clear the area."

Logan blew out a relieved breath and glanced at Skyler. Her jeans were ripped from the fall, and he supposed she'd scraped her knee. At the very least, she'd sustained another bruise. His anger flared at her additional injuries. At the creep who'd just tried to kill her. But Logan wouldn't let her see that he was upset. Not when she desperately needed empathy.

He softened his voice. "That tumble probably didn't help your head any."

"Are you kidding?" A nervous laugh slipped out. "The adrenaline has all but made the headache disappear."

For now. When the adrenaline abated, the headache would come back even stronger, but he kept quiet. There was nothing they could do about it while pinned down.

"I'm sorry I got you into this mess," she said.

"You can't take responsibility for Marty's actions."

"You still think this is Marty?"

"Yes."

"But why the change in M.O.?"

"Everyone's looking for his car, so it makes sense for him to change things up."

"But to attack right outside the sheriff's office?" Her voice shot up. "That's plain crazy."

"Or brilliant, if you think about it. He's got to know you'll let your guard down here."

She shuddered. "And I almost did. If you hadn't pulled me back in or caught the flash just now…" Her voice broke.

Despite a shooter in the woods, he reached back and took her hand.

She started crying. Big fat tears rolled down her cheeks. "What kind of cop cries?"

"A lot of them do." He dropped down and pulled her to his side.

Her crying intensified and despite her ongoing issues with him, he slid his arm around her shoulders. She moved closer and rested her head on his chest. He drew in her unique scent and felt at home for the first time in years.

He was certifiably crazy. A sniper lay in wait for them and he was calm. Peaceful. The kind of contentment he'd often experienced with her. He wished there was some way he could have more of it. Much more.

But there wasn't. Not with the ways things stood now. Not as long as his job came first.

FIFTEEN

An hour later, Logan escorted Skyler into the sheriff's office. He still held her snuggled under his arm, not a hair's width between them. When she'd stopped trembling and her crying had stilled, he'd expected her to push away from him, but she'd stayed put. Warm and soft by his side. Shock still hanging firm in her eyes.

Not the clinical version of shock, but the stunned amazement of nearly losing her life. She was fighting hard to control her reaction. He suspected it would linger and return full force tonight when she was alone. But now? Now she was trying to be a strong deputy. She just wasn't quite able to achieve it, so she leaned on him.

She probably hated relying on him and would rather turn to almost anyone else. But he liked it. Liked it a lot.

Darcie stepped into the hallway. She appraised them both for a long uncomfortable moment. Nothing new. She was most likely upset with his arm around Skyler, but he didn't care. Right now Skyler needed him. He cherished the opportunity to help her and wouldn't release her.

Darcie focused on Logan. "You're the only one who saw the shooter's location, so Jake wants you to join them outside."

Skyler glanced up at him, looking like his leaving was the last thing she wanted right now. "I'll go with you."

He shook his head. "It's not a good idea with the shooter still at large."

She gave a quick nod of acknowledgment instead of her usual feisty argument. For the first time since this whole mess started, he saw total defeat in her eyes. Jake needed him outside, but he couldn't walk away with her feeling so down. He had to offer something to give her hope.

"You can still help by going back to your files," he suggested. "In case this isn't Marty, we'll have a head start on finding out who it really is."

"C'mon, honey." Darcie linked her arm with Skyler's and drew her away from Logan. "I'll help you."

He watched the women, extreme opposites in size, moving as one down the hallway, before he turned his attention to his phone and dialed Wagner.

"Glad you called," Wagner said excitedly and rushed on before Logan could request help. "We got the files from the Rose City Rollers and finally have Nicole's last name. It's Hill. There's also an emergency contact form with a Portland phone number. The contact's last name is Hill, too, but we can't make out the first name. We suspect it's one of her parents."

"Is the phone number still active?"

"No, but we're getting a subpoena for the phone company. Hopefully after we get the account information, we'll find a Hill still living at that address."

Logan tamped down the excitement that started to grow. No point in getting worked up now. It would take time to obtain the subpoena and more time to get the phone company to turn over the information. "Let me know if you need any help obtaining the subpoena. Otherwise, text me after it's been served."

"What did you call about?" Wagner asked.

Logan recounted the shooting. "I'd like an evidence recovery team out here stat. And not just any team. Our very best."

"That'd be Gary Watkins and his crew. You met him at the bank. I'll get them on the road as soon as we hang up."

"Thanks, Wagner." Logan made sure he sounded sincere as he'd come to rely on Wagner quite a bit. "You've proved to be invaluable to me on this investigation."

"I do my best," he said flatly, but Logan still heard that his compliment had hit the mark.

After disconnecting the call, Logan stepped outside, the cold wind biting his face. He crossed the parking lot to Cash, who stood near the woods in conversation with Jake. Though Jake was the squad leader, Cash held himself with such authority no one would know who was in charge from simply looking at the pair.

"Let's get started and catch this creep." The eagerness in Jake's voice spoke to his commitment to Skyler.

A commitment Logan couldn't make, and he appreciated Jake's willingness to look out for her. "Any sign of the shooter?"

"He's long gone," Cash said.

"Any witnesses?"

Jake shook his head. "A pedestrian down the street reported a pickup truck flying out of the alley that runs behind the woods. She saw a male with dark hair driving, but that's all she could give us."

"Then let's see what we can find out here." Logan snapped on a pair of latex gloves and headed toward the spot where the muzzle had flashed.

The scene played out again in his mind. Slowly. In glaring detail. Spotting the flash and recognizing what it meant. That instant bolt of fear. Reacting instinctually and taking Skyler to the ground. The bullet whizzing overhead.

Close. Too close.

He'd almost lost Skyler. His Skyler. The thought made

him nauseous, and he felt what he suspected was a panic attack coming on. He'd never experienced one before, not even with his dad's many tirades.

Calm down. You're no good to anyone this way. Keep it together and find the guy.

Controlling his breathing to slow his heart rate, he stepped gingerly through knee-high grass and large ferns and halted for a moment when he spotted a green object discarded near a tree. He continued on until he could identify the item.

"A rifle sling?" Cash said from behind, confirming Logan's suspicion.

Cash pressed around Logan. He picked up the sling and examined it. "The metal hook's been ripped out." He bent down and ran a finger over the tree. "Looks like the shooter took off in a hurry and caught his rifle on the tree."

"The sling military issue?" Jake asked.

"Affirmative." Cash circled the area, then suddenly squatted and picked up a shell casing. "It's a 7.62 mm."

"Which likely means military," Jake tacked on, probably for Logan's sake.

But Logan had studied weaponry and didn't need to be told that ordnance for rifles listed in millimeters often signified military issue.

Cash bagged the casing. "I doubt we're dealing with a trained sniper. They'd never leave a casing behind."

Jake took the bag from Cash and pocketed it. "But the ammo and the sling could mean our shooter is more likely to have military connections."

"Or not," Cash said. "The sling could have been purchased online or the shooter could simply have stolen it and the ammo in a burglary." Cash held out the sling. "Either way, this sniper attack says our shooter means business and he won't likely stop until he completes his mission."

* * *

Thirty minutes later, Skyler gave up on trying to concentrate. She took a moment to pray for courage to face whatever was coming next, reminding herself that she wasn't alone in this. Not only was God walking with her, so were her teammates. Logan, too, but that wasn't something she was willing to analyze. Not after the way she'd sought his comfort when it was the last thing she should do.

She needed her family instead. Not just Darcie, but all of them. They'd surround her with their warmth and compassion. They'd give her hope and bolster her spirits.

She got up. The throbbing ache of new bruises made her want to drop back into the chair, but she kept going and tugged Darcie to her feet. "The guys should be coming in any minute. Let's go down to the conference room to wait."

Darcie arched a brow but said nothing as she fell into step with Skyler. They passed by coworkers, whose gazes were blatantly questioning. Skyler ignored them and continued on to the conference room, where she found Brady and Archer sitting at the table. Brady was whittling as usual, Archer looking at his phone as they waited for the debrief.

Thankful to see their friendly faces, she gingerly settled in the chair next to Brady. Despite the nearness of her trusted friends, the same sense of contentment she'd found with Logan outside didn't materialize.

Brady winked at her. "Glad to see you're alive and kicking."

Archer fired him a testy look from the other end of the table. "As our not so tactful associate said, glad to see you're okay, squirt."

"I can be tactful," Brady argued.

"Maybe in your sleep," Archer shot back good-naturedly.

Skyler laughed, lightening the atmosphere in the room. She was thankful for their bantering to take her mind off the incident and off Logan.

They continued to occupy her mind until Jake, Cash and Logan entered, each of them sporting grim expressions. So it wasn't going to be good news. Skyler prepared herself for their report as Cash dropped a large evidence bag on the table.

Brady grabbed it and examined the item closely before looking up. "A rifle sling. Military issue."

"Military?" she said slowly and let the military connection roll around in her brain until it jogged her memory. *Finally.* The thing she couldn't come up with last night. "How could I not remember this?"

"What is it?" Logan took a step closer.

"Something's been bothering me since the robbery. I didn't know what it was until just now. It's the way Marty held his gun. He kept his finger alongside the gun instead of on the trigger. As if he'd been taught that our natural instinct is to squeeze and he'd learned to prevent accidental discharges."

"That doesn't sound like an amateur robber who suddenly decides to pick up a gun." Logan's eyes lit up. "More like someone with weapons training and experience."

She nodded. "Doesn't mean he's military, but if you add it to the ammo bag, it makes sense." She continued to ponder the lead, her excitement quickly falling. "It also means if he's former military, he may not have gone to college, and we can kiss the lead on college rings goodbye."

"Lots of soldiers attend college on the GI Bill when they get out." Cash smiled, something he rarely did, letting Skyler know he was trying to make things seem less dire. "Plus it opens a new avenue to pursue. Soldiers often buy military rings that look a lot like college class rings. Maybe that's what you saw."

"Good thought," Logan said enthusiastically. "After my team finishes processing the scene, I'll ask them to add military rings to their search."

"Wait. Why's your team processing the scene?" Skyler shot a questioning look at Jake. "This happened in our own backyard. Why aren't we taking point on the investigation?"

"Don't worry, squirt. It'll be a joint effort." Jake's lips tipped in a soothing smile. "We all kinda like having you around, so I figured it wouldn't hurt to have the fed's forensic team give us a second look in case we missed something."

"Not likely," Brady grumbled. "We're as good as or even better than a team of suits."

Jake shot him an irritated look, and Skyler's mouth fell open. It looked like Logan had completely won Jake over. How on earth had he done that? Winning her over, Skyler could understand because it involved her heart, but Jake? Mr. Logical and By the Book?

Darcie stood, drawing everyone's attention. "Let's not forget Skyler was on the way to the doctor when this happened. Since I can't add much to the investigation, I'll work on getting an appointment for her. That way we can minimize the time she's exposed to the killer."

"Or I could just not go," Skyler said, not wanting to miss any part of the investigation now that it seemed to be heating up.

"Not an option," Logan said forcefully.

"I agree." Jake triple-teamed her. So much for the earlier smile. "I doubt our shooter is anywhere in the vicinity, but if there's any chance that he is, we'll need secure transport."

"I'll request one of the bureau's unmarked vans," Logan offered. "Skyler can ride in the back unseen. We can take her home in it, as well."

Jake nodded. "Good. Do that."

As they worked out the details, Skyler sat back and didn't say a word. What was the point in arguing? The entire squad seemed to be in agreement, and if she'd learned anything in her eighteen months with them, it was that trying to buck the general consensus was like trying to climb a hill in an ice storm. You took a few steps forward but would soon slide backward even farther.

"I'll go call the E.R. now." After a lingering look at Skyler, Darcie left the room.

Jake came to his feet. "Let's finish this debrief and get Skyler to the doctor."

Still standing, Logan rested his palms on the table and leaned forward. "Before we do, I want to mention that we've learned Nicole's last name is Hill. Her emergency contact on file with the Rose City Rollers listed a Portland phone number. Unfortunately, it's been disconnected. We're subpoenaing the records. If we're lucky, a Hill family member still lives at that address."

Skyler's hope blossomed. "Wonderful news."

Jake peered at Logan. "I've played nice and left this investigation to your team. As I just told Skyler, that ends now. Going forward, I want to know what you learn the minute you learn it."

Logan returned Jake's stare. "I don't have a problem with that as long as we don't get in each other's way."

"Translated," Case said dryly, "don't get in the suit's way, but he may get in ours."

Brady snorted. "Typical suit behavior."

Skyler had to give Logan credit. He didn't seem fazed by their jabs at all.

"Do you want to sit around and talk about me?" he asked. "Or should we discuss the military implications of the sling?"

Archer sat up. "Skyler and I have both negotiated several hostage situations that involved soldiers in the past few years." He turned to Skyler. "Maybe after this shooting, you should prioritize your records search on military incidents."

"Couldn't hurt, could it?" Cash asked.

"No."

"Sounds like a good idea to me," Logan said.

And just like that, the squad agreed with Logan yet again, frustrating her when they sided with him. She thought about pointing out how the man they were agreeing with was the same one they'd slammed as a suit several times, but the shooting had zapped all her strength. And arguing wouldn't change anything.

Besides, the adrenaline keeping her going had all but disappeared. What little energy she had left, she had to reserve for a review of her files in case Marty wasn't the creep who'd just escalated his desire to end her life.

SIXTEEN

Logan bid farewell to his team after they finished going over the crime scene with a fine-tooth comb. They'd gathered very little useful evidence. That could change when they processed the casing and sling. At least he hoped it would change. Hoped they'd find something—anything—to move the investigation forward. Until then he'd latch on to any lead they uncovered and run with it.

He returned to the small conference room to check on Skyler's progress. She'd insisted on continuing to search her files while she waited for the van to be delivered for her trip to the doctor.

"Any success?" He tried to sound cheerful as he took the seat next to her.

"Maybe." She looked up and rolled her neck. "Three possible military standoffs fit the bill. Two of them are strong enough to pursue."

Though Logan still liked Marty for the attacks, he settled into his chair and gave her his full attention. "Tell me about them."

She pulled a folder from the small stack and slid it over to him. "The first one is Sam Vaughn. He's a former soldier. Three months ago he had a mental break and took his family hostage."

Before opening the file he asked, "You think this guy's capable of violence against you?"

"No, but even if I did, he's in jail. I do think his brother, Zac, who's also former military, is not only capable, but sufficiently motivated."

Intrigued, Logan wanted to look through the folder, but he'd give Skyler a chance to give him the details first. "Tell me about Zac."

"I negotiated the standoff with Sam, which is when I met Zac. He believed he could talk Sam down by himself and didn't want our squad to interfere. He figured if he didn't involve the police, he'd keep his little brother from having a record."

"Sounds like a reasonable request for a brother to make, though I know your team couldn't accommodate it."

"Zac didn't understand that. I tried to comfort him by telling him if Sam surrendered peacefully his mental illness would likely get him transferred to a psychiatric hospital instead of spending time in jail." She shook her head in sad little swings. "I was wrong. Somehow Sam managed to fool the psychiatrist who evaluated him and was found competent and in control of his faculties. The judge declared Sam a danger to the community. He sentenced the poor guy to five years."

"Ah," Logan said, understanding the motivation now. "Zac blames you for his brother's sentence."

She nodded. "He stopped by here to talk to me one day, but I wasn't on duty. He left a bunch of verbal threats to pass on. A few days later, he started sending abusive letters. They arrived every week for a while. They're in the file. He definitely was angry enough to take it out on me."

Logan scanned the letters. They held words like *death, revenge* and *retribution.* Each letter escalated in tone. He noted the last of six letters was date stamped a month ago.

"It seems odd that he went silent for a month and is suddenly choosing to act."

"I agree, but he's still a good possibility."

Logan concurred. "And the other guy?"

She tapped the next folder in the stack but didn't give it to him. "This one is older. Happened about a year ago. Roger Felder came home from Afghanistan experiencing mental health issues. He ignored the warning signs until one morning he woke up with his hands around his wife's throat."

"That'd make most men sit up and pay attention."

She nodded. "He voluntarily checked himself into the hospital for a psychological evaluation. That's where things went south. While there, he relived a bombing attack and took a nurse hostage. I was called in and negotiated a peaceful surrender."

"Nice to hear these things do sometimes end peacefully."

"Actually, they end that way more often than not. You only hear about the ones that go wrong on the news." She fingered the cuff of her vivid gold-and-black tunic as if searching for something soft to comfort her through her stress.

The sadness in her face tugged at Logan, and the urge to console her nearly had him reaching out to her. Like he had outside. Draw her close and hold her. Make promises he wasn't ready to keep, just to rekindle that feeling of home. To feel like a part of something, of someone again. But he couldn't promise her anything other than he'd find the man trying to kill her. That's what she needed from him. Nothing else.

He swallowed down the urge and gestured at Roger's file. "How did this guy come to have it in for you then?"

"After he surrendered," she said, seeming completely oblivious to the war going on in Logan's mind, "he was committed to the psychiatric ward on a psych hold. Since he'd come in voluntarily, up to that point he could have left at any time. But now he was forced to stay, and he needed to get out. His wife was pregnant. He couldn't work from the hospital, meaning they were getting behind on bills, and he blamed me when they wouldn't discharge him."

"Any threats after that?"

"No."

"Which guy do you like for this more? Zac or Roger?" Logan kept his voice calm. Not an easy thing. Not when his desire to make both men pay for threatening her nearly had him jumping out of his chair to hunt them down.

"Zac," she replied. "Don't get me wrong, though. Roger was mad. Good and mad. But despite his fragile hold on reality, he didn't seem as upset as Zac. Maybe deep down he knew he'd benefit from the treatment."

"We need to find out if he's still in the hospital to rule him out."

"My squad can handle finding him."

Logan reluctantly nodded his agreement. He wanted to take on the task himself—go after these guys—but her team needed to help her, too, and he had to let them participate. "What about the third case you mentioned?"

She rested her hand on another folder with tattered edges that made Logan think it'd been handled many times. "It's not really viable. This guy isn't alive anymore and I've never received a threat from any family members."

"So why mention it?"

"It was the first time I soloed as a negotiator." She looked at her knees and started unraveling a thread from the hole in her jeans. "You know how you never forget your first real incident on the job that ends badly? The way it lives with you and you keep wondering if you could've done something differently?"

"Yes," he replied softly.

"Yeah, well, this one ended about as badly as it could

have." She paused and took a breath. "After this guy was arrested, he committed suicide in his holding cell."

Logan slid closer to gain her attention. "You can't feel responsible for anything that happens once the standoff ends."

She looked up, her wounded expression cutting him to the core. "I know, but sometimes I can't let it go."

After everything she'd been through this week, he didn't want to make her relive this case if she didn't have to. "Tracking down the first two guys while chasing Marty will strain our resources. If none of these leads pan out, we can come back to this one. Until then, I think we're better off focusing on the first two. Deal?"

"Deal." She glanced at her watch. "I've got another hour before my doctor's appointment. I'll use that time to track Zac Vaughn down and maybe we can go see him afterwards."

Logan opened his mouth to refuse, but she held up a hand. "Don't bother to say no. If you do, I'll go without you."

"You think you can ditch me that easily?" he asked half-jokingly.

"I know I can." She stared him down.

He didn't doubt she could slip away from him if she put her mind to it, and he knew when to give in. Still, he'd have an agent scope out Zac's place. Only then would he let her go anywhere near the potential killer. And she wouldn't be going alone, of that he would make certain.

Logan pulled into the gravel driveway leading up to Zac's house, which looked like it came straight from a horror movie. Logan's sixth sense screamed to take care. He slowed by Agent Johnson, who'd had eyes on Zac's place for the past few hours.

Logan lowered his window. "Zac home?"

Johnson nodded. "Been there this whole time."

"Anyone else?"

"A woman—driver's license says she's his wife—and a boy. Maybe a middle schooler. The age of Vaughn's son. I didn't see anyone else."

"Stay alert and watch our backs." Raising the window, Logan slowly eased down the drive.

By the time he shifted into Park, Zac Vaughn was stepping onto his front porch, his arms crossed over a barrel of a chest. He wore a faded flannel shirt and torn jeans with untied work boots. He was in as much disarray as his ramshackle porch.

Logan glanced back at the windowless portion of the van where Skyler sat. "You can come up here to look out the window while I check things out," he said, knowing she was going to balk. "But promise me you'll stay down and in the van until I signal it's safe."

She sighed out a long breath.

She was upset. He got that. The doctor had denied her request to return to active duty. Logan supposed her frustration was valid. They couldn't seem to catch a break on the investigation, and her health issues complicated everything. But no matter how cute she was when her lower lip came out in a pout as it was doing now, he wouldn't jeopardize her safety.

"I'm sorry, Skyler," he said, making sure to let her know he understood her situation. "It's the best I can offer."

Resignation settled into her eyes. "I promise to stay here." She slipped up front and took the passenger seat.

After one last look at her to be sure she meant it, Logan climbed down and headed across the yard.

"No need to come any closer." Zac's booming voice reverberated through the trees. "I don't want whatever you're selling."

Logan fished his credentials out and displayed them as he continued forward. "Special Agent Logan Hunter, FBI."

"I didn't do whatever you're here to blame on me."

When Logan got close enough, he visually scanned the guy for a weapon. He'd like to frisk Zac, too, but he had no grounds to do so. "I'm here to talk to you about your brother, Sam."

His eyes narrowed. "Something happen to him?"

"No. Nothing like that," Logan said looking around the area for any threat. "I want to talk to you about how you feel about his incarceration."

Zac seemed to relax and leaned back against the door-jamb. "Don't like it. End of story."

"I…" Logan crooked a finger for Skyler to join them. "*We* have a few questions for you."

Skyler jumped from the van.

Zac trained his full attention on her as she joined them. Recognition suddenly broke on his face. He scowled and came to his feet in a defensive posture. "What's *she* doing here?"

"Like I said, we want to ask a few questions about your brother."

"I'm not talking to *her.*" He started to turn away.

"Wait," Skyler called out. "I got your letters."

"Yeah, and you did nothing about them just like you did nothing about Sam." His lip curled. "You promised he wouldn't go to prison. Next thing I know, he's serving five years. So why should I listen to anything you've got to say?"

"The judge made the decision. There was nothing I could do."

"Is that so?" he snarled.

"Yes," she answered.

He crossed powerful arms. "You could've at least tried to talk to the judge. Maybe testify at the sentencing hearing. But no. We never see you again after the trial and Sam goes away with common criminals." He shook his head sorrowfully. "A man who served our country. Saw his buddies die and lost a bit of his mind. Stuck behind bars with lowlifes."

"I'm sorry," she said and Logan could see she was buying into this guy's story and taking on a boatload of guilt.

"Sorry doesn't cut it. You need to pay for what you did." He curled his fingers into a fist. "I still want to kill you with my bare hands."

She shivered, and Logan knew it had nothing to do with the decidedly colder temperatures.

Logan moved closer. "I could arrest you for threatening a law enforcement officer."

He let his gaze travel over her. "You could, but then looks to me like she's not on duty. Plus, she never identified herself as a law enforcement officer. How was I to know she still is one?" He grinned, revealing tobacco-stained teeth.

Logan fisted his own hands to keep from throwing Zac against the wall. "Suppose you tell me where you were yesterday morning, last night around seven and again this morning about ten."

"Suppose I don't."

"Then I'd have to bring you in for questioning."

"Why don't I save you all that trouble?" That sarcastic grin returned. "I'll get my lawyer over here. Then see what questions you have a right to ask me."

Logan gritted his teeth before saying something he shouldn't. The guy had threatened to lawyer up before Logan could even ask a real question. They wouldn't get anything out of him. Continuing to try would be a waste of time.

"We'll pass on that conversation for now," Logan said. "But this isn't over." He took Skyler's arm and backed toward the van, never taking his eyes off Zac.

Skyler took her seat in the rear and stared at her feet. Logan suspected she was struggling with the guilt Zac's allegations raised. Logan wished he could do something to help, but she'd have to work through it on her own.

His phone chimed with a text, then rang with a call.

Wagner's icon appeared on the screen, and Logan accepted the call first.

"Olivia was able to provide enough detail for a decent sketch of Marty," Wagner said. "You should've just gotten a text with the artist's rendering. After your approval, I'll distribute it to the authorities."

"Hold on while Skyler takes a look." Logan thumbed to the picture and climbed between the rows of seats to show it to her. "Does he look anything like Marty?"

She studied the screen for a long time, then blocked part of the picture with her fingers. "If I hide the nose and cheeks, yeah. The shape of his head, the jaw and the eyes are all the same." She passed the phone back to Logan.

"Distribute it, Wagner," Logan said as he returned to the driver's seat. "And get it out to media outlets, too."

"Will do."

"And be advised that I'm leaving Johnson here to keep an eye on Vaughn."

"Are you sure you want to do that?" Skepticism was rampant in Wagner's tone. "It'll take a necessary resource away from our investigation."

Wagner was right. Having one less agent working their leads would delay the hunt for Marty. And would delay Logan's promotion. He felt confident in his ability to protect her—did he really need Johnson on this, too?

He glanced at Skyler in his mirror. Her gaze met his and held. His heart somersaulted in his chest. Logan wouldn't change his mind. Johnson would keep tabs on Zac. Logan would even dedicate other resources to Skyler's safety if needed. Protecting her had to come above everything else.

Even if it means you don't get the job. The thought didn't catch him by surprise after the past few days, and he honestly wasn't as upset as he'd suspected he'd be.

SEVENTEEN

That evening, Skyler mounted the last corner of a welcoming banner for the Christmas party in the firehouse's entryway and looked out the window. The forecast for the next few days called for freezing temperatures and snow. Snow. White, fluffy, sparkling snow would set the perfect backdrop for the Christmas party. *If* the roads were cleared, allowing guests to get to the firehouse. A big "if" in the Portland area with few resources to deal with a heavy accumulation, putting the party in jeopardy.

She offered a prayer for the event and for everyone's safety as she climbed down from the step stool. She looked up to find Logan assessing her, much as he'd been doing all day. "I can't stand you watching me that carefully."

"Sorry." He set down his laptop and joined her. "I'm trying to figure out how you're doing after our visit to Zac. Looked like you were feeling kind of guilty over what happened to Sam."

"I'm sad about his incarceration, but I know it's not my fault," she said. After working through Zac's accusations that afternoon, she truly meant it. "Even if I wasn't okay, I decided to put everything, even Marty, out of my mind and enjoy putting up the last of my decorations." She grabbed a bag of red and green balloons.

"Can I help?" he asked, sounding uncertain.

Skyler shot him a questioning look. "You want to stay?"

"Yeah."

"Honestly? You want to put up decorations?"

"Yeah." He sounded like he was getting annoyed at her questions, but she had no idea why.

She didn't want to make him madder, but she also didn't think it would be a good idea to work so closely together on something unrelated to the case or her protection. "You've already devoted so much time to me. Don't you have something else you should be doing for the investigation?"

"I can do it later." His tone was flat, hollow almost, and his eyes held the same sadness she'd seen in the kitchen last night.

She should say no to him, but she knew that lost look. Knew how it felt. She smiled to let him know she welcomed his help. "You're sure?"

He flashed an easygoing smile. "Absolutely."

He was actually putting her ahead of work again. Or maybe putting her charity ahead of work. What should she take from that? She had no clue, but she was still sure it wasn't a good idea to let him stay. Not for her peace of mind anyway.

Searching for an answer, she glanced around. Having him here with the Christmas decorations surrounding them brought back their first Christmas together. A joyful, wonderful time in her life. The feeling completely erased the memory of Zac's brutal anger today.

"I suppose you can stay," she said quickly before she changed her mind.

Logan threw back his head and laughed, the warmth of his happiness reverberating off the high ceiling.

"What?" she asked, confused.

He grinned at her. "Your invitation couldn't be less enthusiastic."

She felt her ire rising. "And that makes you laugh?"

"No, but it was fun to watch you argue with yourself and lose the argument." He took a few steps closer. "Reminds me of when we went ice-skating at the Lloyd Center. I had to work hard to get you on the ice."

She'd never forget that first time she'd skated and couldn't stifle her grin. "I fell so many times. You kept picking me up and dusting me off. And never even teased me about my klutziness."

He came closer still. "Mentioning that the toddlers on the rink were skating better than you would've been mean, don't you think?"

"So that's what you were thinking, huh?" She socked his arm.

He took her wrist and drew her close. "I loved that day. The way your cheeks turned red in the cold." He brushed his thumb over her cheek. "Seeing your determination despite falling all the time. And I especially liked how you let me kiss you each time you fell. So you see, I wasn't at all sorry you were such a klutz."

She should step back, but she was mesmerized by his eyes. By the magnetic pull that always existed between them.

"I…" Emotions scrambled her brain, and she couldn't continue.

"Me, too," he said on a whisper, then lowered his head to claim her mouth.

His kiss sent her senses into a dizzying spiral. She couldn't breathe. Couldn't think other than to know this was perfect. So perfect. They'd always been perfect together from the first day.

She gave in and let herself feel. Let herself enjoy the kiss while it lasted…which wasn't long.

He suddenly lifted his head. "I'm sorry. I shouldn't have." He looked contrite and frustrated at the same time. "As you said, nothing has changed, and I don't want to lead you on.

It's just… I still…" He shook his head. "I may not be free for a relationship, but my feelings for you haven't gone away."

Her first instinct was to run. Fast and far away from him. From the way he made her feel. But she wasn't the type to run from her problems. Better that they face this head-on.

"I understand," she said.

He shot her a surprised look. "You do?"

She nodded. "You've put me first in many ways the past few days, and it's not hard to see you care about me."

"You're right. I do. But that doesn't change things for me." He shook his head again. "I still need that promotion. I know that makes me incredibly callous and selfish. Thanks to you, I can see that now, but I can't give up on the job."

She should've expected his answer but she'd foolishly hoped he'd changed. Still, he'd made progress and that might mean he was ready to take the next step. "You don't have to give up on the job. Really you don't. Just take a closer look at your priorities. Let this thing with your dad go." She lifted a hand to touch him, but decided it would be a bad idea and let it drop. "You'll be surprised at the relief you feel. Trust me—I know. I did it with my own parents."

He searched her eyes for a long time before shaking his head. "I wish it was that simple."

"I never said it was simple. It took me a long time to get over the hurt they caused, but it's worth it."

He released her and backed away, his expression saying he wasn't ready to believe her.

She instantly felt cold without his arms around her. And colder still at the knowledge that while he did truly care about her, it still wasn't enough.

Under gray morning skies, Logan bid Nicole's parents goodbye and stepped onto their stoop while Skyler said a more protracted goodbye in their foyer. Wagner had really come through today, obtaining the phone records for Nicole's emergency contact, then tracking down her parents. Logan should be ecstatic about the lead, but the discomfort between him and Skyler left him uneasy.

Every time he looked at her, the kiss came flooding back and he felt guilty for giving in to his emotions. He had no right to kiss her. She needed him to protect her and find the guy trying to kill her. That's it. There and only there was where his attention needed to remain.

Remember that.

He scanned the area carefully. Up the tree-lined street. Down it. Looking for any threat. Thanks to hourly text updates from Johnson, Logan knew Zac wasn't lurking in the shadows, but they'd learned that Roger had been released from the hospital and still lived in town. Logan hadn't had a chance to check him out.

After talking to the Hills, Logan believed even more that Marty was Skyler's attacker. They'd said he was a druggie who'd been arrested in the past and had corrupted Nicole, turning her against them. They also thought he might've been in the military. Unfortunately, they didn't know his last name. And they hadn't seen Nicole in over a year and couldn't provide any information except her old address. She'd recently moved in with Marty and hadn't told them where to find her. They'd tried to track her down, but her old building manager said she didn't leave a forwarding address.

Logan heard the door close behind him as Skyler joined him.

She buttoned her jacket and huddled against the howling wind sweeping down the street. "I'll never get used to making a death notification call."

"No one ever does." He was glad he rarely had to do them.

"It's even harder when they haven't seen their child in so long." Skyler shook her head. "Marty seems like a real low-life. Turning her against her family that way." She glanced at skies that threatened snow any moment, then after a shake of her head, she started for the van. Logan walked beside her and opened the sliding door.

"You know." She climbed in and settled on the bench seat in the back. "Since the Hills said Marty wears a ring, it'd be great if you could rush the pictures of military rings to show to them, too."

"I'll put pressure on my staff to get them to us by day's end." He closed the van door, then hurried around the front. His phone chimed with a text from Agent Johnson.

Zac's on the move with his son. Has a large duffel. Looks like weapons. I'm tailing him.

After Logan climbed behind the wheel, he looked in the rearview mirror to see Skyler as he updated her.

"We should join Johnson," she said excitedly.

He shook his head. "We don't even know if Zac's involved. Now that Nicole's parents gave us her social security and Oregon driver's license numbers, we're better off heading to my office to track her information down and see if we can find any ties to Marty."

"You're right," she said, sounding disappointed.

He didn't blame her. He'd like to do something other than search records on a computer, too. To make something happen on this case. But meeting Johnson probably wouldn't accomplish anything.

Logan pointed the van toward his office. He'd barely gotten out of the Hills' subdivision when his phone rang from its holder on the dash. He glanced at it.

"It's Johnson again," Logan told Skyler, then put it on speakerphone.

"Zac was carrying all right," Johnson said excitedly. "He stopped at a firing range."

"Interesting." Logan let the news settle over him. An

idea flashed into his brain. An idea that could support or eliminate Zac as a suspect. An idea Logan wouldn't waste time thinking about, but would immediately put into action.

EIGHTEEN

Since it was broad daylight, Logan waited undercover in a stand of trees until Zac departed the firing range, his son trailing behind. Logan had already arranged for Johnson to tail Zac so Logan ignored the guy's departure and turned to Skyler.

"You know the plan." He held up the rifle he'd borrowed from Johnson. "You're a novice and I brought you to the range to teach you to shoot."

"Don't worry. I've got it. Though it'll be hard to fake ignorance when I'm a crack shot." She wrinkled her nose and Logan was glad to see the possible lead had cheered her up after the death notification call.

He smiled at her. "I doubt we'll actually get to shoot, but if you do, channel a helpless little girl."

"You mean instead of the incredibly confident woman I am." She winked at him.

His mood elevated by hers, he stepped into the building and spotted a wizened older man standing behind the counter, eyeing them. Logan was suddenly glad he'd thought to ditch his suit in favor of the jeans and T-shirt he kept in his go bag.

"Help you folks?" Suspicion crept into the man's tone.

Logan supposed it came with the territory of being surrounded by guns and gun-happy people.

Logan casually slung his arm around Skyler's shoulders. "I want to teach the little lady how to shoot." He got a jab in the gut at the "little lady" comment, and he had to fight hard not to smile. "My friend Zac—Zac Vaughn—recommended this place."

"You just missed him."

"He was here? Today?"

"Left no more than five minutes ago."

"Man." Logan took his arm from Skyler and dramatically ran his hand over his face. "Been a bad week and I would've really liked to skunk Zac on the range today. What was he shooting?"

"HK G3," he said as if challenging Logan's weapon knowledge.

Logan recognized the military issue rifle. It was hard to come by for civilians, but not impossible to steal. It fired the same caliber bullets as the slug they'd found outside the sheriff's office. Logan played it cool and held up his gun case. "I much prefer my Remington to the Heckler & Koch."

A flash of respect lit the old guy's eyes. "They're both respectable weapons. I'd have liked to have seen the two of you compete."

"There'd be no competition." Skyler poked Logan in the biceps. "This guy has to be better than everyone at everything."

Logan hated that she spoke the truth. He'd once been proud of that fact, but after the past few days, he could see how he paid the price for it.

"Zac's a hard one to beat," the old man said.

"Too bad he's not here for me to prove you wrong." Logan moved to the next phase of his plan. "I don't suppose you'd tell me which shooting station Zac used so I can see if he left any of his targets behind. That way I can harass him about wide shots the next time I see him."

"Rifle area. Lane five." He gestured at a door to his

left. "Since you're so eager, go on in. We'll settle up when you're done."

"Thanks, man." Logan all but ran for the door to the shooting stations.

At lane five, Skyler scooted in front of him. "Now will you tell me what you hope to accomplish here?"

"After seeing the way Zac let his house fall apart, I hoped he was sloppy and would leave his casings behind."

"To compare them to the one recovered at my office."

"Exactly." Logan snapped on latex gloves and squatted to search the dark corners for casings, but he came up empty-handed. "Nothing."

"Hey, don't sound so disappointed. At least we now know he owns a weapon that fires a 7.62 mm like the casing we found at the office."

"Plus the HK G3 is a military issue weapon, but neither of those points give us any evidence to bring him in."

"What we need is an actual slug he fired today." Skyler peered down the long lane. "The only way we'll get one is if the owner shuts down and lets us retrieve the bullets in the traps. Even then, we'd be hard-pressed to prove a recovered slug came from his rifle."

"True, it won't hold up in a court of law, but at least it'd give us the probable cause for a warrant to search his house." Logan gestured toward the door. "Let's go talk to the owner."

"But what can you tell him to make him comply?"

"It'll have to be the truth."

"Then he'll know you lied to him before."

"Can't be helped," he said and led the way back to the retail area.

The proprietor looked up. "Don't tell me she picked it up that quickly."

Logan explained the true reason for the visit and apologized for misleading him. "I'd like to gather the slugs at the end of lane five."

The old man crossed his arms. "I won't betray a fellow vet for any reason. You want the slugs? Bring me a warrant. Maybe I'll still have them by the time you do."

"You'd destroy evidence?" Logan clenched his jaw.

He smirked. "Didn't say I'd destroy anything. Just saying I hope we haven't cleaned out the traps like we do on a regular basis."

Logan thought about ignoring the man. Ignoring legalities and rushing back inside to grab the slugs, but that wouldn't help the investigation at all.

"Let's go," Logan said to Skyler. When they got to the door, he reached out to stop her. "Let me check things out first."

She remained inside and he stepped into the brisk wind. The gray skies mimicked his mood perfectly. He made his way across the front of the building and past parked cars. Each shadow, each dark space brought to mind pictures of Zac as Skyler's stalker. Him hunkering down in the woods by the parking lot. Training his gun on her. Squeezing the trigger. The bullet whizzing through the air. Piercing Skyler's body. Her falling to the ground.

Logan could hardly breathe for thinking about it, and he suddenly knew how much she mattered to him. That she'd once again changed his life for the better. Stepping away from her after they put her stalker behind bars would be even more difficult now than it had been the first time.

Thankful to be home after a long day, Skyler unlocked the front door as Logan stood watch. All afternoon, they'd both been silently engrossed in their own thoughts while they completed record searches on Nicole. Now, Skyler's mind was on the call she'd just received from Jake.

The paint sample on Darcie's car confirmed the red Jeep

was a 1997 model. After updating the vehicle alerts, Jake had assigned a team to run all Jeeps fitting the added criteria, hoping it would lead to a registration record with an address for Nicole or Marty.

After striking out at the firing range, Skyler was thankful for the progress, but she was also exhausted from poring over Nicole's financial records and needed a break from it all.

She set her purse on the table. "I'm going to make a pot of tea. Would you like some?"

Logan snorted. "Tea, are you kidding?"

She hadn't forgotten he didn't like tea. She was simply trying to lighten the mood. It clearly hadn't worked, so she set off for the kitchen.

"Stop!" Logan jumped forward and jerked her back by the elbow.

"Hey, I got it. You don't want tea. No need to react like a crazy man." She tried to slip her arm free, but he held tight. Frowning, she peered up at him. His face had hardened into granite and his eyes narrowed into slits as he continued to grip her arm.

A cold knot of fear tightened her stomach. "What's wrong?"

He drew her toward the door. "There's a trip wire strung across the entryway."

"A bomb?" she squeaked out as she spun to get a look at this wire for herself.

Silvery thin, it was strung tautly from wall to wall about a foot from the floor. Less than three feet from where she'd just stepped.

Only three feet from death. Her death.

NINETEEN

A tangled rush of relief and rage threatened to take Logan down. But he wouldn't let that happen. Not now when Skyler needed him to stay vigilant. The trip wire could be a ruse to get her out in the open for another sniper attack. He couldn't let that happen.

He phoned Jake. Then, after making a careful sweep of the surroundings, he hurried her inside the coffee shop across the street. He completed a quick threat assessment before seating her as far from the window as possible. He forced her to drink some water and alternated his focus between the door and Skyler, watching for any symptoms of shock.

She stared out the large window, not uttering a word. When the FRS command truck pulled to a stop out front, she bolted from the coffee shop. He rushed after her and remained at her side until they reached the truck, and the squad came charging out the back.

Brady and Archer immediately cordoned off the area, while Cash started setting up the robot. Jake barked orders to evacuate the area over his microphone to patrol officers whose cars were screaming onto the scene. Darcie did what she did best, enveloping Skyler in a quick hug.

"Oh, sweetie," she said, then led her up the steps into the truck.

As much as Logan wanted to be with Skyler at this time, he needed to pace and couldn't abide the truck's confined space, so he updated Cash on the street.

"Give me a minute to deploy the robot and we'll soon know if we're dealing with a bomb." Cash worked quickly, yet carefully, while Logan stormed back and forth, his mind filled with the close call. Filled with visions of an explosion and the world going black.

Cash moved the robot onto the street. "Okay, that's it from here. Time to send this bad boy inside and watch on the monitors." He headed for the truck.

Despite Logan's distaste at the prospect of the claustrophobic space ahead of him, he had to see what the trip wire connected to. He followed Cash into the truck. Cash dropped into a chair and maneuvered the controls, sending the robot into the firehouse.

The space seemed airless as Logan took a spot behind Cash. Jake joined him, his face ashen. Darcie and Skyler huddled on the bench. Darcie spoke soothingly to Skyler, and she seemed to be regaining some color in her face.

Never had he felt so helpless. So out of control.

He heard Cash take a deep breath and hold it. Apprehension gripping Logan, he swung his gaze from Skyler back to the monitor to see the robot rolling up to the trip wire. Cash changed the robot's direction to follow the nearly invisible wire, then bent forward and squinted into the monitor, his finger hovering over the controls and stopping the robot.

He sat back and let out a slow whistle. "It's a rudimentary bomb, but there's enough C-4 here to do some serious damage. Anyone within the blast radius wouldn't have made it out."

"Oh, no… If Logan… Oh, no." Skyler panted as if she couldn't catch her breath.

Darcie drew her closer.

Logan understood her feelings. Felt them to his soul. If

not for that brief sun break, the rays glinting on the wire, they'd be...

"Rudimentary means you take care of it yourself without a squad, right?" Jake asked, tension obvious in his voice.

Cash nodded. "But we should increase the evacuation area just to be safe."

"I'll get the uniforms to expand the perimeter," Jake said and started talking in his microphone.

Looking fiercely focused and controlled, Cash donned a drab green suit with a rigid ballistic panel covered in flame-resistant Nomex and body-protecting Kevlar. He opened a tool kit and evaluated every item. Checking and double-checking. His slow, precise movements were fitting for a bomb expert, his concentration unparalleled.

Cautious was the word that came to Logan's mind. A control freak. The opposite of the daredevil Skyler had made Cash out to be.

He snapped the case closed. Before he stepped out the door, Skyler jumped up and grabbed him in a hug. "Be careful, Cash."

"Don't worry, squirt. This is a piece of cake," he said, extricating himself as if the hug embarrassed him.

He exited the van, then lumbered across the street and into the firehouse. They all watched on the monitors as he bent over bricks of C-4. The tension reminded Logan of the bank standoff. Except this time, Cash was the one at risk. Skyler was safe.

Something Logan kept thanking God for. He hadn't prayed in a long time, but the bomb had affected him deeply.

A sudden cheer went up in the truck, and Logan swung his head to look at the monitor, catching Cash's thumbs-up.

"He disabled it." Tears of relief rolled down Skyler's face.

"Is it safe to go inside now?" Darcie asked.

"Not until Cash sweeps the entire building," Jake replied. Skyler jumped up and hugged her team members. She paused by Logan and looked as if she might hug him, too, then moved on.

He was an outsider. Once again an outsider.

Not just with her and the squad, but with everyone. He was alone, looking in at others as they lived in the present while he could only think about the future.

Sure, he was part of a team that worked well together and accomplished goals. But it ended there. He wasn't part of their personal lives and they weren't part of his. They weren't there for him. Didn't rally around in times of stress and strife as this squad did with Skyler. This squad brought joy and happiness to each other every day and made life much richer.

His phone rang. Thankful for the interruption to his thoughts, he stepped outside to answer Johnson's call.

"You can rule Zac out," he said excitedly. "I felt bad about losing him so I went to talk to him and his wife answered the door. She gave me alibis for each time Deputy Brennan was attacked. I've checked them out. They're solid."

"You're certain."

"Yes, but even if I wasn't, she handed over his rifles. I had them tested and ballistic reports say they're not a match for the shooting at the sheriff's office."

Despite Johnson's initiative, Logan couldn't praise the guy. Visiting Zac was a rogue move and Johnson's actions could've caused dire consequences to the investigation if Zac had been the attacker.

"I'll have a written report on your desk before the day is out," Johnson added.

"See that you do." Logan let his tone convey a word of warning. As Johnson hung up, Logan heard the guy sigh.

Maybe Logan had been too hard on Johnson. Going rogue or not, he'd eliminated Zac as a suspect and they wouldn't be wasting valuable resources. They couldn't afford to be shorthanded when they still hadn't discovered Nicole's address, the significance of the ring or even the makeup connection in Hollywood. Now they had a bomb to deal with, too.

He turned back to the truck to see the squad members pouring out.

Jake, his usual tight expression on his face, stopped by Logan. "It's clear to go inside. We'll be looking at the suspects to see who has experience with explosives. I assume you'll be joining us."

Logan nodded and trailed the team across the road to the firehouse. Inside the foyer, Skyler's feet stuttered to a stop near the trip wire location, her hand flying to her chest. Cash had removed the wire, but she appeared frozen in place. She'd held it together so far, but the incident had impacted her. Deeply.

Logan's heart broke for her, and he needed to be closer to show his support. He made his way through the group and stopped behind her. He laid both his hands on her shoulders and drew her back against him. That earned him a raised eyebrow from the squad, but he chose to ignore them and focus on Skyler. He hoped she'd feel his warmth. Feel how much he cared about her. Feel his strength of will to protect her.

"I think we could all benefit from sitting down," Darcie suggested. "C'mon, honey. Let's go to the family room." She took Skyler's arm.

Logan suspected Darcie was more interested in getting Skyler away from him than sitting down, but he couldn't prove it.

"Wait," Brady said, rushing inside with a box in his hand. "We shouldn't even be in here, but at the very least we need to don booties so we don't mess up this crime scene."

They each grabbed a pair, and Logan was shocked that he'd required the reminder. He'd been so filled with concern for Skyler that protocol hadn't even crossed his mind. But he still wasn't going to stop them from entering their sanctuary after such a terrible shock.

They went into the family room, their booties whispering over the polished concrete. Still too anxious to sit, Logan stood as close to Skyler as possible, ready to help her if she needed him, while the others sat.

"Before we get started," he said. "We can scratch Zac off the suspect list." He recounted his conversation with Johnson. "That leaves Marty and Roger."

"Okay." Jake's brows creased as he looked at Cash. "Our first step is to figure out if either one of them has experience with bombs."

Cash jerked the quick release tabs on his suit and shrugged out of the top. "Anyone with basic demolitions experience could've built this one."

"Could this strengthen our theory of a military connection?" Skyler asked.

Cash nodded. "There's no better place to learn demolitions than in the military. But this might not have been the work of an expert. Most anyone who served would know about this type of booby trap."

"Couldn't someone also have found plans online?" Logan asked.

"Of course."

Jake planted his hands on his waist. "So what you're saying is this doesn't really narrow down our suspect list at all?"

"Didn't say that," Cash snapped. The event had clearly taken a toll on him, too. "Whoever set this trap needed a source for the C-4. With C-4 pretty much limited to the U.S. military and some government entities, a nonmilitary suspect could only get the C-4 illegally. If the suspect is a military demolitions expert, it would be easy for him not to have used everything he was issued for maneuvers or training and have a cache on hand."

"Dude, you're totally confusing me," Archer said. "So we *are* looking for a demo expert then?"

"Not necessarily," Cash replied. "Could just be someone who knows an expert willing to share their supply of C-4."

"So it could be Marty or not." Skyler sounded beaten.

Archer sat forward. "We may not know much about Marty, but we do know Roger Felder is former military. It would help to know if he has demo experience giving him easy access to C-4."

Skyler jumped up. "His file's in my bag on the hall table. Let me grab it."

Logan really wasn't eager for another suspect vying for their attention, but if Roger had demo experience, it would make him a prime suspect and they couldn't ignore him.

Skyler rushed back into the room, and shoved the open folder at Cash. "Roger was a combat engineer, whatever that means."

Brady and Cash both pulled in hasty breaths, and the room went still.

"What?" Skyler's gaze shot between the two men.

"Means he not only has experience," Brady offered, "but it was his job to blow things up. He's a viable suspect of the highest order."

"Wasn't he hospitalized for some sort of mental breakdown?" Archer asked.

Skyler nodded. "But he was released a few weeks ago."

Jake met Logan's gaze. "I got a call back on one of my leads this afternoon. Roger was diagnosed with schizophrenia."

Before Logan could really process the implications of a mental illness being thrown in the mix, his phone rang with a call from Wagner.

"I have to take this. It's my office." Logan stepped toward

the foyer, but an insane need to keep Skyler in view nagged at him, so he stayed close enough to keep an eye on her.

He lowered his voice and answered.

"The L.A. office called," Wagner said. "They've talked to the manager at Nicole's last address. As the Hills said, she didn't leave a forwarding address, but mail suddenly stopped coming. The manager thinks she forwarded it through the post office. I've already got a subpoena in the works for post office records. If she moved in with Marty, this'll give us Marty's address. From there we should be able to learn his full name."

Logan's optimism made an appearance again. "Be sure you call me the minute they come through with the request." He disconnected and returned to the group.

"I'll go see Roger first thing in the morning," Cash was saying.

Skyler jutted out her chin and straightened the collar of her blouse as if straightening out her thoughts, too. "I'm coming with you."

"That's not a good idea," Logan jumped in. "He sounds far too unstable for you to risk it. I'll go with Cash."

She crossed her arms. "I'll be fine. Roger wouldn't have been released if he wasn't stable and on medication."

"I won't allow it, Skyler." Logan shot her down without apology.

She pulled her shoulders back in a hard line. "He's suffering from a mental illness. He won't be easy to communicate with and my training and education make me the best person in this group to get through to him."

"I concur," Cash said.

Logan fired an irritated look at the guy. But he supported Skyler, and Logan had no choice but to agree. "Then let's at least change up our mode of transportation. Skyler can ride with Cash. I'll drive the van as a decoy. When I'm sure I haven't been followed, I'll join you at Roger's house."

"That'll work," she said. "Though I don't think you really need to join us. Cash and I are more than capable of handling this on our own."

"I'll be there." He looked away before he got mad and made additional demands.

He was peeved that she didn't want him around, when he should be happy that she had this amazing team on her side. They could provide her not only with emotional support, but with their wide range of abilities that went beyond the average police officer's skill set, they could also keep her safe.

She doesn't need me. The thought hit him like a ton of bricks. She had a life without him.

Then it struck him.

This kind of life had been his for the taking for years. Was his for the taking now. If he could only change his focus as Skyler suggested. He wanted to change. Wanted it badly. But he also wanted the promotion and couldn't quit hoping *it* would finally achieve what he'd spent his whole life thinking he couldn't live without—his father's approval.

Skyler watched Roger carefully in the hazy morning light. His disheveled appearance and the indicators of paranoia obviously meant he'd stopped taking his medication. Not unusual for people with mental health issues. Yet, despite his evasive behavior and wild look, Skyler felt safe standing between Cash and Logan.

"Why do you want to know where I was?" Roger sent furtive glances into the distance.

Cash took a step closer to Roger. "Someone's trying to kill Deputy Brennan and you've threatened her in the past."

Roger eyed her with the same hostility she'd seen at the standoff. "'Course I did. I want her to pay. She's evil. She had me locked up. She should die." He continued to ramble as if she weren't standing two feet from him. His wild gaze darting everywhere at once. "I could do it. Now. Right now.

Yes. Now." He grinned. "I got a whole stockpile of weapons inside. Yeah, that's right. A whole pile of them."

Skyler took Roger's ranting with a grain of salt, knowing it was the illness talking. But Logan seemed furious that Roger's crazy rambling alone didn't give them probable cause for a search warrant or a reason to arrest him.

"Would you like to show us your guns?" Logan asked.

"You in my house? No. No. Not in my house." Roger shook his head so hard his cheeks slapped. "It's mine. My house. No. Not you." Skyler suspected Logan's formal dress made him seem intimidating to the disturbed man.

"How about me, man?" Cash asked. "I mean, fellow vets have got to stick together, and I'd really like to see your stuff."

"You a vet?" Roger ran a hand over hair that hadn't seen a comb or shampoo in some time.

Cash nodded. "Army."

Roger gave Cash a quick once-over. "No. Army wears uniforms. Blue ones. Not like yours. You're a cop." He jerked his head at Logan. "Like him."

"I am now, but I served just like you. In Afghanistan."

Roger shook his head again. "I gotta go. Must go now. Right now." He darted back inside and slammed the door. The firm click of the dead bolt echoed through the silence.

"So much for that." Cash shook his head sadly as they walked to his car. "Man. It's hard to see a brother suffering like that."

Skyler agreed. She had to help the guy. "As soon as I get home, I'll call Roger's doctor to let him know he's off his meds."

"So now what?" Cash scrubbed a hand over his face.

"He threatened Skyler in an offhand way." Logan shrugged out of his suit coat and carefully laid it on the passenger seat of the van. "Gives your team some leeway in running him in and getting him another psych eval."

"After all he's been through, I'd rather not arrest him and put him through more trauma." Cash turned to Skyler. "You're the one affected by this. What do you think?"

"I agree with you. Roger shouldn't have to suffer additional stress unless we at least have enough evidence for a search warrant."

"We have no choice." Logan kept flexing his hand as if itching to act. "If he's the guy stalking Skyler, we can't let him wander around."

Cash stared at the house. "Why don't I hang out here to keep an eye on him? I'll make sure he doesn't come after Skyler and maybe I can find a way to help him."

"Without meds, he won't likely respond to you," Skyler warned.

"Then maybe I can get him to check back into the hospital."

Skyler didn't think that was likely, either, but she applauded Cash's caring heart. "I'll ride back with Logan. I'll call you after I talk with Roger's doctor."

Logan's phone chimed. After glancing at the text, he held it out to Skyler. "It's the military rings."

Eager to follow up on another lead, she scrolled through the list. The fifth ring sent her pulse racing, and she stabbed a finger at it. "That's the ring Marty wore."

Cash looked over her shoulder. "That's an Iraqi Freedom Ring."

"So Marty *is* military?" Logan asked.

"Anyone can order a ring like this and have it custom designed or even buy a used one. But, yes, I'd lay odds on him being military." Cash locked eyes with Skyler. "And if he served in Iraq, be advised that gives him skills—deadly skills—we haven't even begun to discuss."

TWENTY

"Nicole's parents confirmed the ring Marty wore was the same one you picked out." Logan pocketed his phone and looked at Skyler, who was fixing lunch in the firehouse kitchen.

She looked up from spreading mayo on thick wheat bread. "It's a start, but it'd help if we could actually figure out his identity."

"Why don't I follow up with Wagner on the post office subpoena to see where it stands?" he offered. "That's our best chance right now of learning his full name."

Logan didn't wait for an answer. He dialed Wagner and started pacing. He'd been doing far too much sitting around of late and he felt antsy. He went into the family room and stared out the window.

"Any word on the post office records?" he asked the minute Wagner answered.

Wagner huffed out a frustrated sigh. "I talked to them this morning. They said they'd have them to me by now."

"Text me the contact person's information and I'll get on their case."

"Okay," Wagner said, but Logan could tell he was disappointed Logan needed to step in. "FYI, we got a call on the Jeep. A woman saw the news bulletin and claims the

Jeep's been abandoned on a rural road on the east side. Not sure if it's legit, but Unger's on his way over there now."

"Call me as soon as he determines if it's the vehicle we're looking for."

Buoyed at the sudden good luck, Logan hung up. He waited for Wagner's text with the post office contact information, then dialed the number and identified himself as the agent in charge of the case.

"Before you go off on me," the harried woman said, "I was about to email the data to Agent Wagner."

"Great, then you won't mind copying me on it, too." Logan gave her his email address and went back to the kitchen to tell Skyler the good news. He found her on the phone.

"It's Cash. He's calling about Roger." She set her cell on the island. "You're on speaker, Cash, so Logan can hear."

"You'll never guess who showed up at Roger's house." Excitement lingered in his voice.

"Who?" Logan asked, half dreading the answer.

"The squad."

Skyler's head shot up and she locked eyes with Logan. "You mean the FRS?"

"Yep. Roger placed a nine-one-one call claiming he'd taken a hostage."

"And does he have a hostage?" Logan asked.

"No one went into his house, and he didn't come out while I was watching. I suppose it's possible he abducted someone before we talked to him. Archer's getting the throw phone ready. Hopefully we'll know something soon."

"We're on our way," Skyler said.

"No!" Logan and Cash shouted at the same time.

"No," Logan said, softer. "This could be a ploy to get you over there so Roger can take a potshot at you."

"I agree," Cash added. "It's best to wait there."

"But—"

"The post office is emailing Nicole's information to me as we speak," Logan rushed on, hoping to get her excited about staying put. "We can go through the file while we wait to hear back from Cash. Plus we may have found Marty's Jeep. Once it's confirmed, we need to be ready to head over there."

"Really?" Her eyes lit with enthusiasm.

He nodded.

"Call us as soon as you know anything, Cash." She hung up and set a sandwich in front of Logan. "We should eat now so we'll be ready to go."

He climbed onto a stool and took a bite of the thick ham and Swiss sandwich before opening his laptop to check his messages. He spotted the USPS return address. "Email's here."

Skyler came to stand behind him. He was aware of her closeness. Could feel her warmth. Smell her fresh scent. But even that wouldn't distract him from learning Marty's address and maybe his real name.

"There." He stabbed a finger at the screen. "Nicole's mail was forwarded to a William Anderson III in an L.A. neighborhood not far from her previous address."

Her gaze flashed to his. "You think Marty's real name could be William?"

"I hope so."

"The Hills said he'd been arrested." She took over Logan's laptop and started typing. "I'll connect to the county's database to see if he has a rap sheet. If so, we can confirm the name and picture."

Logan let her take charge and pull up the record for William Anderson III. Logan took another bite of his sandwich and as the window opened, he swallowed hard. She tapped the screen, bringing his focus to the photo of a male in his early thirties.

"Oh, yeah," he said, shooting a fist up. "William's middle name is Martin."

"And his mug shot looks exactly like his sketch." She thumped her finger on his picture, then looked up at Logan, her eyes luminous with excitement.

Logan smiled at her. Moved to draw her in for a celebratory hug, but remembered his place in her life and stopped. "Looks like we finally have an ID."

"William Anderson III," she said as if trying the name on for size. She focused on the screen again. "He's been arrested for drug possession a few times, though nothing in the last year. He also served in the army in Iraq, specializing in EOD."

"Explosive Ordnance Disposal," Logan said.

She looked at him, her eyes wide, a smile playing on her lips. "Marty's our guy."

"Looks like it." Logan ignored the continuing urge to hug her and jerked his gaze away. He reached for his phone. "We need to get an alert out on him."

She grabbed hers, too. "It'll be faster if I do it."

Logan's phone rang under his hand. Spotting Wagner's icon, Logan quickly answered.

"The Jeep's registered to a William Anderson III," Wagner said before Logan could get a word out. "And you'll never guess his middle name."

"Martin." Logan resisted letting his joy loose in a whoop of laughter.

"How'd you know?" Wagner sounded disappointed.

"Post office records. Text me the address for the Jeep and we'll head over there." Logan hung up and looked at Skyler. "Hurry up with that alert. We've got a Jeep belonging to one William Anderson III to process."

On the deserted country road, Skyler circled the red Jeep—pausing at the dented front end. She ran a gloved finger over streaks of silver paint. Residual anxiety from the crash returned, sending her pulse racing. She swallowed it down and breathed deep until she regained her focus.

"Looks like a match to Darcie's car," Skyler said, stepping back.

"It'll be easy enough for the forensic lab to confirm." Logan pulled open the passenger's door. "Let's see what the interior holds."

From the driver's side, Skyler rifled through items in the middle. Loose change—pennies mostly—gum wrappers, an empty cigarette pack. Nothing of interest until a napkin in the cup holder caught her eye.

"Check this out." She held it out for Logan. "It's for a motel bar in a seedy part of Portland. He could be staying there."

"I'll call and confirm."

She shook her head. "It's a known drug hangout and they'd give you the runaround on the phone. We're better off going there once we finish up here."

"We should get a uniform over there in the meantime to keep an eye out for Marty."

"I'll call it in." She backed out of the car and dialed dispatch. Normally she'd route her request through Jake, but Cash had called on their way over to say Roger hadn't taken a hostage. He'd escaped through a side window before the squad showed up, and they were now involved in a manhunt.

After making her request, she and Logan completed the search before heading to the motel. They arrived at the low-slung building with chipped paint and crumbling sidewalks as a flurry of snow began falling from dark skies. A county cruiser was backed into the lot where the deputy could watch the entire place.

Logan parked in front of the office. "You're off duty so let me ask the questions."

Not wanting to be the cause of some legal loophole when

this case went before a jury, she nodded. "Let me tell the deputy he can take off before we head inside."

She stopped at the car and the deputy reported no suspicious activity. She sent him on his way, then followed Logan into the lobby. It smelled like stale cigarettes and orange-scented air freshener. Logan went straight to the desk clerk, an elderly man who looked as tired as the motel.

With the patrol officer gone, Skyler watched the parking lot. Fast-food wrappers skittered over the cracked asphalt leading to a rusted-out Dumpster, where she was sure they'd find used needles and other drug paraphernalia. Light flurries continued drifting toward the ground and even the promise of the fresh white blanket didn't improve the place any.

She saw movement on the upper balcony. A man fitting Marty's build stepped from a room near the end. It was too much to hope that it could be this easy to find him, but her heart kicked into gear anyway. He turned and walked toward the office. Nothing about the guy's build ruled him out, but his face was shadowed by a black hoodie and she couldn't make a positive ID.

He reached the stairs and turned.

Please look up. Please.

He paused. Stared across the lot.

His face was a direct match for Marty's driver's license. Her heart started galloping.

"It's Marty," she shouted at Logan and reacted like any cop would, charging out the door. She reached for her weapon before she remembered she was off duty and her gun was in her purse. She fumbled for it on the run.

Marty looked up and recognition dawned on his face. He barreled down the stairs and flew across the parking lot. If he was carrying, he didn't draw his weapon. He had a head start and rounded the end of the building, disappearing from view.

She heard Logan coming after her. Protocol said she should let him take over, but she wouldn't end her chase and risk Marty's escape. She managed to free her weapon as she charged for the end of the building. Gun at the ready, she shot around the corner. Logan called out for her to stop.

No way was she stopping now.

A hand chopped into her arm, sending her gun clattering across the pavement. She caught a quick look at Marty's drug-crazed eyes before he threw her to the ground.

She landed on her back, her breath knocked from her body. Marty jumped on top of her and wrapped his fingers around her throat.

"Stupid cop," he screamed, spittle flying everywhere. His hot, angry eyes locked on her, but they didn't seem able to focus. "I decide to let you live and you still don't know when to leave things alone."

"Let me live?" she tried to ask, but she couldn't squeak out a word as his grip tightened.

She clawed at his fingers and tried to pry them free. Didn't happen. The drugs made him crazy strong. Her vision started to darken. She was losing consciousness.

Marty got in her face. His teeth even more hideous, his breath more disgusting up close. "Bye-bye, Dep-u-tee. This's the end of the line for you."

TWENTY-ONE

Panic curdled Logan's blood. He'd seen Skyler disappear around the end of the building, but she'd had a significant lead on him. He had to get to her. Now! He pushed himself to run harder, faster, pumping until his lungs felt as if they might burst. He rounded the corner. His heart stopped. Marty straddled Skyler. His fingers were wrapped around her neck, her face red, her eyes bulging.

Rage claimed Logan's core. Roaring like a lion, he rushed to Marty and clamped his arm around the creep's neck, cutting off his oxygen. Marty thrashed and let go of Skyler, lifting his hands to free himself as Logan had hoped he'd do.

"Choking isn't much fun, is it?" Logan growled at Marty as he searched Skyler's face for life. She was so quiet and still that Logan's heart lurched.

He was desperate to check on her, but first he had to eliminate the danger. Flattening Marty on the concrete, Logan jerked his arms behind his back. As he snapped cuffs on the loser's wrists, Logan heard movement next to him. Was it Skyler?

"Skyler," he called out. "Are you okay?"

"Ha!" Marty sneered. "I did her in."

"No, he didn't." Skyler's voice was scratchy and weak,

but simply hearing it gave Logan's body a surge of adrenaline.

"Can you call for a uniform?" he asked.

"Yes," she said, her voice no more than a whisper.

Logan jerked Marty to his feet. "We'll book this loser. Then we can get to the bottom of this once and for all."

"In your dreams," Marty said. "I ain't saying a word."

While Skyler talked to dispatch, Logan pressed Marty's face against the wall. Not because Marty would take off, but because the creep had assaulted Skyler and deserved this treatment.

Pocketing her phone, Skyler joined them and looked Marty square in the face, a desperate fury in her eyes. "Well, William Anderson III." She paused and Logan knew it was for Marty to process the fact that they'd learned his name. It didn't seem to faze him.

"You said something about deciding to let me live," Skyler continued.

"Did I?" Marty smirked.

"You know you did."

He shrugged.

She moved closer to him and Logan was proud of her strength. "Were you talking about your failed attempts to kill me?"

"Who me?" He laughed.

She planted her hands on her hips, looking like a fierce warrior. "Don't play dumb, Marty. If you didn't try to kill me, then why does your Jeep have front end damage with paint from my friend's car?"

Marty's lips turned up in a sick smile, infuriating Logan, who shoved him harder. "It'll be easier for you if you tell the truth now. Lie and I'll make sure you pay all the more."

"I didn't do nothing, man."

Logan knew he was lying, but he couldn't force him to

confess. Maybe he could catch him in one of his lies. "If you didn't intend to kill Skyler, why stay in town?"

"I was waiting for Nicole's funeral."

"If that's true, why haven't you contacted Nicole's parents?"

His mouth dropped open, and his foul breath made Logan gag. "Are you kidding? They hate me, and they'd gladly turn me in. So I kept an eye on the internet, waiting for information about her service."

"And your car just happened to get banged up?"

"Fine. I mighta accidently bumped into the dep-u-tee one day. Maybe followed her another day, but that's it. I swear."

Logan figured Marty wouldn't cop to the more serious bombing and sniper charges without a full-fledged interrogation at the office.

Sirens screamed toward them. Perfect timing.

Logan jerked Marty from the wall. "Let's go."

Skyler led the way, and Logan pushed Marty toward a uniformed officer climbing from his car. Once Marty was secured in the backseat, Logan turned to Skyler. "You believe him?"

"You mean about only ramming me?"

Logan nodded.

"No, but I do think he was being honest about sticking around for Nicole's service." She looked up at the rooms on the second floor. "It might help us figure out if he's lying about the rest if we locate a rifle in his room."

"I'll get the key." Logan left Skyler with the officer. On the way to the office, he phoned Wagner and requested he hightail it over there so Logan could take Skyler home. The FBI office wasn't far away and if Wagner ran his siren, he'd be there by the time they finished searching the room.

Logan went inside and pinned the desk clerk with a don't-mess-with-me look. The guy must've thought better of arguing and handed over the key Logan requested without a fight.

Back outside, Skyler gave Logan a pair of latex gloves and booties for his shoes before heading up the stairs. The stench of stale food and dirty clothes assaulted him the moment he opened the door. He hated bringing Skyler into a place like this, but she simply slipped on her booties and snapped on her gloves, then started going through Marty's things. Logan followed suit. She soon dragged a bag from under the bed and set it on the ratty floral bedspread.

"That's the bag he used in the robbery." Logan went to stand next to her as she unzipped it.

She pulled out three small stacks of cash. "Not much left. The rest of it probably went for living expenses and drugs." She opened the bag wider. "His handgun's in here."

"Then it's pretty certain he'll go away for this last robbery at a minimum." Logan frowned. "But he needs to pay for hurting you, too. Let's turn this place upside down for the rifle and any bomb-making supplies."

Logan let his anger fuel him and had the place thoroughly searched in record time, but came up empty-handed.

"It's not surprising we didn't find anything." Skyler frowned. "Makes sense that he wouldn't want to be caught with the rifle or any bomb paraphernalia in the place where he's living. Not that I think he's clearheaded enough to behave logically."

Logan appraised her. "Are you saying you doubt he's behind the bombing and sniper attack?"

"No. I still like him for that, but I won't let down my guard until we find concrete evidence."

"And until Roger's apprehended, too," Logan added. "C'mon. Let's get out of here and let the forensic guys have at it."

On the walkway, she ditched her booties and gloves. They headed to Logan's car, where Wagner waited for them.

As Logan brought him up to speed, Skyler climbed into the car. She seemed to collapse onto the seat, worrying Logan.

"She doesn't look so good." Wagner stated the obvious.

"Marty nearly choked her to death. I'd make her go to the hospital, but she'd argue." Logan would make sure Darcie completed a thorough exam though. "I want this entire place searched. Call me if you find anything."

Logan got behind the wheel, and sensing that Skyler didn't want to talk, they drove to the firehouse without a word. Several team members' cars were parked in the driveway, which meant once Logan saw her safely inside, he could leave.

Leave for perhaps the last time. Sure, he might see her when Marty's case went to trial, but that was it.

He turned to her and she peered up at him as if she didn't have the strength to go on. He took her hand. She didn't fight him, and he couldn't take his eyes from the woman who always managed to get through his defenses. He didn't like the thought of a lifetime without her.

He gently touched the red welts on her neck. "Marty will pay for this. I'll make sure he goes away for a very long time."

She didn't say anything. Just kept her eyes fixed on his.

He lifted his hand to her face. Slid it into her hair. Drew her closer and waited for her to pull back. When she didn't, he kissed her. Slow and gentle, yet filled with every emotion racing through his body.

She pulled back, her eyes awash with concern. "I suppose this means you'll be getting the promotion."

"Looks like it," he said, wondering what caused her unease.

"You'll be moving back to Portland then." She smiled. "I'm glad. That'll be nice."

Was she hinting that once he moved, there was a chance that they could be an "us" again? And what about his father's approval? Could getting the ASAC position finally allow Logan to let go of it all—to be free to commit to her?

The possibility, even the tiniest of ones, that she might give him another chance was enough to make him want to lay his cards on the table. "We should get together to talk about what coming back here might mean for us."

She looked shyly at her lap. "I don't have any plans tonight if you want to get together then."

His phone rang, and he decided to ignore it. "Tonight sounds good." His phone kept ringing.

"You should get that," she said. "It could be Wagner with something he discovered about Marty."

Logan grabbed his phone from the dash. "It's Inman."

"Maybe he's calling to offer you the job."

Logan thought it more likely he was calling with a problem.

"What are you waiting for?" She pushed the phone toward his ear. "Answer already."

He did without taking his eyes off her.

"Congratulations. We've got our man." Inman sounded cheerful, alleviating Logan's concerns. "We might have a few loose ends to tie up, but the team's already celebrating."

"Too bad I'm not there to see it," Logan said, though honestly, he was content right where he was.

"You'd just get a big head. The team's singing your praises. Saying you managed the investigation like a pro and they'd be glad to work with you again. A real team leader, they say." Inman paused for a long moment, but Logan didn't know how to reply so he didn't respond.

Inman continued, "A man who's out for himself alone would've held his cards close to the vest and not let the team participate as fully as you did. And that makes you a team player and a leader. Just what we're looking for in an ASAC."

Logan mumbled his thanks, but he knew he'd probably

let the team take so much on because he'd felt compelled to devote his time to Skyler.

"So the promotion is yours."

Logan looked at Skyler and mouthed, "I got the job." Her face beamed with the same happiness he was feeling. Did that mean she really was leaning toward giving him a second chance at a relationship?

"I've scheduled a press conference for tomorrow at four o'clock to update the public on the collar," Inman went on. "I'll announce your promotion at the same time."

"Why wait?" Logan hated that he sounded so eager for the news to be announced, but he didn't want to delay hearing his father's excitement when he learned of Logan's success.

"Timing. It'll put us on the six o'clock news to garner the publicity our team deserves."

"But why tomorrow?" Logan looked at the clock. "We could do a four o'clock press conference today."

"Down, boy." Inman laughed. "There are those loose ends I mentioned, and I want them tied up first. The last thing I want is to make a premature announcement with the press and have it come back to bite me."

"Give me a list of what you want done. I'll get on it immediately."

"We need conclusive proof that William Anderson and Clyde are one and the same. We'll need a DNA sample from Anderson, and we'll have to use a private lab to rush the comparison with the blood recovered at the bank."

"Okay." Logan's mind was already running through the possible labs he could call.

"Same thing with the paint found on Marty's car. I'd like to prove Marty attempted to kill Deputy Brennan. Though it's not necessary for our robbery case, it'll boost our public image to show how you saved the life of another law enforcement officer. I also want you to draft a press release.

If you can manage to incorporate Brennan's charity in the piece, it wouldn't hurt to have the bureau appear in the same story as a charitable event."

Logan was surprised Inman even knew about the party, but then he was all about putting spin on his work so it shouldn't surprise him. He felt like Inman was using Skyler for his own gain, and Logan didn't really want to go along with that until he discussed it with her first.

Inman must have picked up Logan's reservation as he asked, "Is something wrong?"

"No," Logan said firmly.

"Good. I want to get the press release out to the media first thing in the morning. Have it on my desk by ten tonight for my review. Also, plan to say a few words at the press conference tomorrow. Nothing elaborate but something befitting our new ASAC. Any questions?"

"No."

"We don't want to mess this up, Hunter. Call me if you think of any."

Logan immediately started running through everything he had to do before the clock struck ten. He'd have to work straight through dinner, and even then it might be a challenge to get it all done. But he wouldn't fail Inman and risk losing the job he'd just gained.

He stowed his phone and turned to Skyler.

"Congratulations." She sounded excited for him. "This makes our talk even more important."

"About that." Logan looked at her. "I'll have to put that off until tomorrow night. Inman's given me a number of tasks to complete today."

"Of course," she said quickly, but her smile vanished. "I'm not really up to it anyway." She pushed open her door and climbed out.

He hurried after her, having to slow down when the

smooth soles of his shoes slipped on the snow covering the driveway.

She opened the door and stepped into the foyer before turning back to him. "Thank you for getting me safely home. Now hurry on back to the office. I wouldn't want you to screw up your new job."

"What's wrong?" he asked, confused at the change in her mood.

She glared at him and the day he'd left her years ago came back in a flash—along with the realization of why she was so angry. She thought he was putting his job ahead of her again.

He was, but only for one night. "Skyler, I—"

"Goodbye, Logan." She closed the door in his face, and he couldn't help but think this was a forever kind of good-bye.

TWENTY-TWO

Skyler spent the rest of the night and part of the next morning ignoring Logan's phone calls and text messages.

"You're such a fool," she mumbled as she looked over her garden in the light of day.

Why had she considered for one moment that Logan might have changed? One call from the boss and he'd ditched her to go running to the office.

She touched her fingers to her lips and remembered their kiss. The kiss, that at the time, she'd thought had cemented his feelings for her. She'd thought it was a new beginning for them—a start to having more in life than her job and friends.

Suddenly she wanted it all.

A husband. Family. Love. Everything that had always been out of her reach. She'd hoped this time with Logan it would've been different, but he'd let her down again.

Too bad.

She'd pick up the pieces. Move on. Find a man who loved her unconditionally.

Yes, that's what she'd do.

Resolve straightening her shoulders, she headed for the kitchen. Before she even took a few steps, the anguish of losing him again took her down, and she sank onto the sofa.

She was simply fooling herself. How would she ever

move on when it was painfully clear that her heart belonged to Logan alone?

She couldn't give him another chance, and she couldn't mope around the house all day, cringing whenever her phone rang.

She had to do something. Anything to keep busy. Gardening always helped.

Thankful her headache had abated, she pulled a jacket from a hook and jerked on snow boots. Even with the snow piling up, she grabbed a large pruner and attacked zebra grass, pushing away the fluffy mounds of snow and sheering it off at the base.

She didn't look up until the wind howled around her and whirlpools of snow whipped into her face, making it hard to see her work. She put her tools in the shed and trudged in the side door.

She heard sounds coming from the family room, likely Darcie waiting to pounce again and discuss Logan. Skyler wished Darcie would just go to work, but with Roger still in the wind, Jake wouldn't take any chances on leaving Skyler alone—even though being alone was exactly what she needed.

She glanced out the window and decided to shovel the driveway. So what if the snow swirled around her and filled the spots she'd cleared. It would keep her mind off Logan and Darcie at bay. She headed for the garage to retrieve the shovel.

"I wondered when you'd come inside," a man's gravelly voice came from the shadows.

She jerked back at the unfamiliar voice. A tall man with a linebacker build stepped from the shadows. He wore work boots, a tattered wool jacket and a ski mask that he lifted from his face. He was an older man, maybe in his sixties, and she didn't recognize him.

She started to back away.

"I wouldn't move if I were you, Deputy Brennan." He pointed a handgun at her.

He obviously knew who she was. That meant this wasn't some random burglary.

"Is this about Roger?" she asked, coming up with the only explanation that made any sense.

"Of course. I should've expected it." The man sneered. "You don't remember me. It would take someone 'warm and caring' like the press claims you are to remember me." He arched a bushy brow and looked at her for a long moment. "You're not like they're saying, are you, Deputy? You step all over people when it suits you, and you're as far from a hero as they come."

"I don't know what you mean. If this is about Roger—"

"Doesn't matter. We can talk about it on the drive."

Drive? "What drive? Where?"

He lifted a satchel from the floor and dumped supplies on the hall table. Handcuffs, duct tape and rope spilled out. She noted his hand, which she'd first thought was covered in an odd glove, was a prosthetic hand. She searched her memory for a man with an amputated hand, but no one came to mind.

He grabbed the cuffs and came toward her.

"Wait," she cried out, panic creeping over her like fingers from the grave. "What's going on? What do you want?"

"Sit," he said.

"No, I—"

He jabbed the gun into her chest. "Cooperate or I'll shoot your little friend I've tied up in the other room."

"Darcie?" Skyler called out.

"I gagged her so she won't be able to answer." He laughed. "Now sit and put your hands behind your back."

She dropped onto the hallway chair. He snapped cuffs on her wrists and pressed duct tape to her mouth. Just like Darcie? Maybe. With only one good hand it seemed unlikely that he'd gotten the drop on Darcie, but Skyler couldn't risk him hurting either of them to find out.

He tugged the ski mask into place, then jerked her to her feet. "Let's move."

He dragged her toward the back door, jerking and pulling on the heavy metal cuffs. She saw Darcie tied to a chair on the far side of the family room, her mouth covered with duct tape. Terror lurked in her eyes.

Skyler tried to convey confidence as the man shoved her out of the building, but her fear spiraled out of control. He hauled her to a van and pushed her into the back. He bound her ankles and cuffed her to the side wall, then offered a sickly smile before closing the door with a bang.

Skyler looked around the space for a weapon. Searching, seeking. For something. Anything to free herself.

She had to escape before they reached their destination. She didn't know what he planned to do to her, but he'd let her get a clear look at his face. Not good. She was a deputy. She knew what that meant. He wasn't worried about her identifying him. He didn't plan to let her live that long.

Logan stared at the report he'd created for Inman last night. Logan had met his final goal and he should be feeling good about himself. But he didn't. Not when he couldn't forget the look in Skyler's eyes before she'd slammed the door. He'd royally messed things up with her, and he didn't know if he could fix it.

His phone pealed, and he grabbed it, hoping to see Skyler's name on the display. The caller ID announced his father. Logan could barely drum up enough enthusiasm to answer.

"Dad," he said.

"I heard about the pending promotion." He sounded businesslike and less than impressed, as he always did.

"And?" Logan asked, fishing for a compliment and hating himself for doing so.

"You've accomplished something special." He sounded as if he were talking to a complete stranger.

No congratulations. No "I'm proud of you, son." Just a somewhat grudgingly said statement.

Still, it was more than Logan had ever received from his father and he clung to it, sitting back to wait for that long-awaited feeling of elation to take over.

He felt empty. Emotionally bankrupt.

"I worked hard," he said lamely as if he could fix the ache with a few more words of praise from his dad.

"We all work hard," his father replied, and Logan knew with a certainty that his father would never give him the validation he'd been seeking.

Logan had tried so hard to emulate his father, but what good did it do him?

And then it hit him.

I don't want to be anything like him. Not an empty shell of a person. I want to live. Fully. Richly.

And that meant a wife and kids that he could love and spoil in ways his father never dreamed of. And it also meant Skyler.

"Thanks for calling, Dad," he said. "I've got to go."

Not used to being dismissed, his father sputtered, but Logan hung up. For the first time in his life he felt good about how he'd handled his father. Logan had always sought his father's love. Always failing so he'd substituted goals and accomplishments. To live as his parents had. To live for the things the world had to offer.

Skyler had told him repeatedly how wrong he was, but he hadn't listened and he'd let go of the very thing he'd been searching for.

Love. Her love.

He could see her standing in front of the Christmas

tree, smiling up at him. He remembered the kiss, and the peace he'd yearned for finally filled the void in his heart. He wanted nothing more than to marry her and spend his life making up to her for all he'd put her through.

Hopefully it wasn't too late to tell her how much he cared for her. Hopefully she'd forgive him for being such a fool.

Hopefully.

Skyler listened to the rhythmic hum of the studded tires grating over the snow-packed road. She'd first hoped the weather would slow her abductor down, but he'd been prepared. For the first time ever, she lamented that studded tires and chains were legal in Oregon.

The van suddenly slowed, bumping over rutted country roads, then stopped.

"We're here," the man called out.

She felt the vehicle lighten as he hopped down. He opened the back door and hauled her out. She searched the area. They were out in the middle of nowhere. In a field filled with tall drifts of snow. A narrow trail cut through the mounds of snow, leading deeper into trees as thick as a forest.

No one would find her out here. No one. Her heart fell and panic threatened to take her down.

The man started moving them forward. "I suppose I should tell you who I am before it's too late. Name's Elroy Eaton."

Tony Eaton's father? My first solo negotiation. The poor solider who committed suicide.

"I doubt you remember my son, Tony. You were supposed to get him help for his PTSD, but he ended up doing time and took his life in jail."

How could he think she'd forgotten Tony? The poor man had been so desperate for help that he'd held a psychiatrist hostage at the VA hospital and begged for care. She'd never forget that or his death. She negotiated the standoff, and he shouldn't have done time. But he'd made a mistake. A big one.

He'd threatened the president's life while in his holding cell awaiting a psych evaluation. Threats to the president were taken seriously and carried a stiff federal sentence. One he didn't think he could serve. So he'd ended his life.

If Eaton would remove her tape, she could tell him that, but he continued to drag her through knee-deep snowdrifts toward an older-model car nearly buried in the snow. Even wearing boots, the icy snow settled in, instantly chilling her feet.

He jerked open the driver's door and shoved her onto the seat, then cuffed her to the wheel. As he looked down at her, the snow landed on his dark hair, making him look even older. "I'm sure you didn't have a clue that I blamed you. That I wanted you to pay."

Burning rage darkened his eyes. "How I wanted it. But I didn't believe in the whole eye for an eye thing, so I left you alone. But then..." He paused, fisted his hands and took in a few slow breaths as if he struggled to control himself. "Then these unrelenting stories came on the news. You were a hero. A big hero. Everyone was eating it up. Hero, my eye! Just the opposite. I couldn't let you trick another unsuspecting person the way you fooled my Tony."

A smile slid across his face. "There's only one way to stop you. You must die."

Logan tried calling Skyler again, but she didn't answer. He left another message, then tried to throw himself into his job. Didn't work. She was all he could think about.

He glanced at the clock. Two hours until the press conference. He quickly calculated the time it'd take to get to the firehouse and convince her to talk to him, then get back to the office in time for the press conference.

With the snow coming down hard, the odds were against him, but he didn't care. Telling Skyler how he felt and making up with her seemed as essential as breathing to him.

He made it to his car in the parking garage in record time, then plowed through eight inches of snow to arrive at the firehouse, frazzled and worn-out from the treacherous drive.

The command truck sat in the driveway along with the team's cars. The snow had likely brought them home early. He was so thankful Skyler was inside, toasty warm, not out on these roads.

He trudged through snow to the door, but before he could knock, Jake jerked it open. The other squad members except Skyler stood right behind him. Logan remembered Jake's earlier warning that if he hurt Skyler again, he'd have to deal with five people with guns, but the rifle Brady carried seemed like overkill to Logan.

"Before you say anything, I need to talk to Skyler," he said. "I know she—"

"She's been abducted," Jake interrupted.

"What? How?" Logan's stomach plummeted.

"A man broke in and tied me up, then took off with Skyler." Darcie rubbed eyes red from crying. "I managed to get to a phone and call Jake."

"Roger?" Logan asked.

She shook her head. "He wore a ski mask, so I couldn't be sure at first. But then I noticed his prosthetic hand."

"Roger has both of his hands." Logan's mind raced over possibilities, but he couldn't come up with any. Fear sent his pulse skating higher. "Then who?"

"We figured it might have to do with the third military file Skyler pulled for review."

The one Logan had put off. "But Skyler told me the guy committed suicide."

"That's why we looked into his family instead," Cash

said. "Turns out his dad lost his hand in an explosion in his younger years. We're headed to his house now."

"I'm coming with you." Logan crossed his arms and waited for an argument.

"Then you'd better get your vest." Jake fixed his eyes on Logan, sending a wave of panic through his body. "With so little time to plan, I wouldn't be a bit surprised if this all goes south on us."

TWENTY-THREE

Standing outside Skyler's door, Eaton pulled a laptop from his backpack. "Thanks to that reporter Paul Parsons, no one will know I was behind this and I won't be headed to jail like my poor, poor Tony."

Paul Parsons? What does he have to do with this?

Eaton set the computer on the roof. "His broadcasts tipped me off to the fact that the robber who'd tried to run you off the road likely had a military connection. All I had to do was make sure I left plenty of evidence pointing to someone from the military. You'd waste your time tracking down that connection and no one would ever suspect me."

Thanks, Parsons.

Eaton frowned. "And I'd have been successful in taking you out long before now. If that agent hadn't gotten in the way all the time. But you know…it's turned out better this way. Everyone will know who you really are." That hideous smile returned for a flash before he concentrated on the computer. "Just a few more things to do and you won't make any more promises to helpless people that you won't keep."

He started humming as he dug out a small webcam and clicked a few keys on the laptop. Holding out the camera, he moved his arm around as he watched his computer. "Recording perfectly."

Was he planning to make a video of some sort?

He gently clicked her door closed, then grabbed the computer and went around to sit in the passenger side. Melting snow slid from his hair, but he didn't seem to notice it as he flipped on the overhead light and mounted the camera on the window beside him. "It would've been simpler if I'd been a better shot or even if you'd tripped the bomb at your house. But it's so much more satisfying seeing your face."

No wonder Marty hadn't claimed responsibility for these attempts on her life. He didn't do them.

"There." Eaton showed her the computer screen.

The video from the camera's wide-angle lens recorded her every movement. He removed a timer from his pocket, connected wires running to the back of the car, then pressed a few buttons. The digital screen came to life. She saw the neon-green numbers start a three-hour countdown before he mounted the timer on the window next to her, where the camera caught it, as well.

"I don't suppose I told you about this little baby. Yes, it's for explosives in the trunk. Not very original, I know, but effective. Don't you agree?" He looked at her as if he really expected her to be able to answer him. "I'd rather not give you three hours, but then it allows me time to get back to town and make sure people have plenty of time to tell others about the video. I'd like to see it go viral."

She mumbled against the tape and pulled against her cuffs.

"Now a quick message to explain this all to the viewers." He jerked down his mask and started the video recording. He leaned close to her and she could smell his nervous sweat as he disguised his voice and repeated Tony's story, withholding their names.

"Perfect," he said and slipped out of the car. Once he was out of the camera's range, he removed his mask. "Relax, Deputy. Save your energy to enjoy the big event." He leaned back in, that sick smile playing on his lips again. "Since I'm broadcasting your little performance live on the internet, I can't take the tape off your mouth or you might find a way to summon help. Too bad. The video would be so much more entertaining if you could scream."

Seated in the back of the FRS vehicle with Cash and Darcie, Logan listened to the team recount Tony Eaton's story. Jake drove and Brady rode shotgun. Literally.

Archer sat forward. "Tony's father never threatened Skyler, but it's seeming like he blames her."

"But why now all of a sudden?" Logan asked.

"Maybe all the publicity she'd received lately set him off," Archer suggested.

"So what's the plan then? We go to his house and you use your mad negotiation skills to get her back?"

Cash and Archer exchanged a troubled look.

Logan's anxiety spiraled out of control. "What are you not telling me?"

Cash clamped a hand on the back of his neck. "Eaton was a construction demolitions expert in his younger years. It's how he lost his hand."

The thought left Logan as cold as the storm raging outside. "So he knows bombs and he's got Skyler. He won't likely blow up his own house, which means she's probably not there." At the thought of her at some unknown location in the hands of a bomber, Logan could barely breathe.

"The good news is there haven't been any explosions reported in the city," Cash said. "So if that *is* his plan, he hasn't acted yet."

Logan grabbed on to the positive thought like a lifeline and shrugged into his vest. The squad ran down their plan, which they agreed would have to remain fluid once they saw what they were facing. When the truck slowed to a crawl, Logan moved to the front of the vehicle to look out the window.

"That's our place." Jake stopped in the middle of the road and pointed at a modest bungalow.

Multicolored Christmas lights glowed at the roofline and light shone through the large picture window. The scene looked like an idyllic Christmas setting Skyler would embrace and not at all like the house of a killer.

"Looks like he's home," Logan said hopefully.

Brady lifted his binoculars. "If he took the trouble to put up lights, I doubt he's planning to kill himself, too."

"Which means either he's not using a bomb or she's not here." Logan moved closer to the window to get a better view.

"There's movement inside," Brady announced.

"Most likely Eaton then. His wife is deceased and Tony was their only child." Jake looked at Logan. "How do we want to approach this?"

Approach? "I'd like to storm the place, but we're better off in stealth mode and surprising him."

Jake nodded. "Let me park this bad boy and we'll go in."

Logan waited for one of them to say he was staying in the truck but no one spoke. The men were double-checking their weapons, and Darcie was gnawing on her fingernails.

Jake tossed a headset to Logan. "You're with me. Archer and Cash, you're lead team. Brady, locate a stand with good visibility—if there is any in this storm—and take it. Everyone listen for my directions."

They hopped out of the van, and the blowing snow bit into Logan's face. He prayed Skyler was inside and not somewhere out in the cold, a bomb strapped to her chest.

Archer and Cash crept into location behind a parked car, then signaled for the others to move in. They'd just reached the lawn when a chair was hurled through the picture window, followed by a gunshot blast.

"Down." Jake's command had everyone hitting the

ground as a fresh volley of shots mixed with the keening wind.

"Tell them to hold their fire," Logan whispered frantically at Jake. "If Skyler isn't inside, we need Eaton alive or we'll never find her."

Jake leaned toward his mic, but another round of shots rang out, skipping across the lawn and making Jake dive for cover. The other team suddenly returned fire, and Logan saw Eaton go down.

"No!" Logan screamed. "We need him."

"Hold your fire," Jake yelled, but Logan feared it was too late.

The neighborhood went silent, a barking dog the only sound besides the wind howling over them.

"He's not getting up," Logan said. "We need to go in."

"Agreed." Jake signaled for the squad to advance.

Logan rose, expecting a bullet to knock him down again. Half hoping for one as it would mean Eaton was still alive. But none came. They scrambled up to the front door unscathed. Logan reached for the knob.

Cash grabbed his arm. "Stop. He's a demo expert. This could be a trap."

Logan didn't want to waste time, but he stepped back to let Cash shine his headlamp on the door frame to inspect it. "We're good, but be careful inside and wait for my direction before moving."

Jake met Logan's gaze. "We go on three."

Logan nodded.

"One. Two. Three."

Logan burst through the door and quickly swept the small family room. Eaton lay on the floor. Blood oozing from his chest, his hand pressed to the seeping spot. Logan should be careful and wait for Cash's all clear, but he had to stop the bleeding and keep Eaton alive to question him in the event Skyler wasn't there. He ran to him and kicked his rifle across the room. After holstering his own gun, he grabbed a nearby afghan and wadded it up before dropping to his knees by the moaning Eaton.

"Find Skyler." Logan's words came out in a strangled cry.

"Everyone hold positions except Cash," Jake commanded, standing guard over Logan. "Be quick, Cash, but don't take any chances."

Logan jerked Eaton's hand away and pressed the blanket against his chest. The fabric was soon saturated. "Get Darcie in here!"

"Once the house is cleared," Jake replied, his usual calm tone missing.

"There's no time," Logan said frantically.

"I'll give her a heads-up." Jake tapped his microphone. "Eaton's got a gunshot wound to the chest, Darcie. He's fading in and out of consciousness. Call an ambulance. I'll let you know when it's safe to tend to him."

Logan stared at his bloody hands. Bright red lifesaving blood. He pressed harder. Eaton's eyes flashed open, and he tried to focus on Logan, but Logan didn't think he managed it.

"Skyler—where is she?" Logan demanded.

Eaton opened his mouth as if to answer, then it went slack and his eyes closed again.

"No!" Logan screamed and checked Eaton's pulse. "He's still alive, but barely."

Cash barreled into the room. "We're clear."

"And Skyler?" Logan shot a look at Cash. The shake of his head told Logan everything he needed to know.

Skyler was out there somewhere and the only man who knew her whereabouts was bleeding out and could die before revealing her location.

TWENTY-FOUR

Skyler gave up. Not on being rescued or finding a way out of this car on her own, but on struggling against the panic as she'd been doing for the past hour.

She leaned her head back, closed her eyes and did her best to ignore the icy cold settling into her body.

Father, help me let go of my fear. To be brave and trust You to take care of me. To find that peace You always provide in a time of crisis.

She took deep breaths. In and out. Over and over until blood flowed to her muscles, relaxing them. On a positive note, the cold had taken her mind off the dull ache that remained from her concussion. She opened her eyes to check her watch.

Five o'clock.

Logan's press conference was over and he'd gotten his job. How she wished he'd chosen her instead and was searching for her, but her last words to him made sure he wouldn't come looking for her ever again.

She'd closed the door on him instead of working things out. The very same thing he'd done to her years ago, and she knew how he must feel right now.

She blamed her childhood of neglect. She'd thought she'd worked through all her issues, but obviously they still affected her, much like Logan's past affected him. He'd been neglected, too, by emotionally unavailable parents. But that's where the similarity in their lives ended.

The faith she'd been so fortunate to find through a friend in high school allowed her to take a more carefree approach to life. Logan had decided to control his environment to avoid pain.

In reality, her decision not to open her herself to love had left her life nearly as empty as his.

Something she needed to remedy. And she would.

If she got out of this mess alive—no, *when* she got out— she'd work with him to find a compromise between their lifestyles and their insecurities. Then they'd both find the kind of love and peace she was sure God wanted them to have.

Panic made Logan light-headed as he sat behind Eaton's computer. Darcie and Archer had accompanied Eaton in the ambulance while the rest of the squad searched the house for a lead. So far nothing.

Logan jiggled the mouse to wake up Eaton's computer. The monitor flashed to life and a video playing on the screen caused Logan to gasp.

"What is it?" Cash came up behind him.

"Skyler," Logan managed to get out as he watched her sitting in a car, the windows all around her covered in snow, making him think of a tomb. The overhead light shone down on her, revealing her hands cuffed to the steering wheel. She lay back with her eyes closed. For a moment, he thought she might be dead, but then she moved and his heart soared.

Cash pointed at the screen. "What's that?"

"I don't know," Logan replied, seeing something moving behind her.

"Increase the video size."

Logan clicked the mouse and the video filled the screen.

The object in question was an electronic clock with a timer underneath counting down from ninety minutes.

"You think he put a bomb in the car and we're already too late?" Logan asked, panic threatening to take him out.

Cash sucked in a breath. "Time is current on the clock. We have ninety minutes to rescue her."

Logan jumped to his feet, knocking the chair to the floor. He jerked off his tie and started pacing. "We have to find her."

"Then you need to calm down," Jake said as he and Brady joined them to watch the video.

Logan took a few deep breaths, but he didn't feel even the slightest bit more in control.

"We're now looking for anything that will give us the car's location." Jake sounded imposing, but Logan saw his hand tremble. "Let's tear this place apart. Brady, you take the upstairs. I'll finish this floor. Logan and Cash, keep on the video to see if there's anything in it that might give us the location." Jake eyed Logan. "You good to do this? If not, I'll take over."

"I'm good." Logan hoped if he spoke the words, they would actually become true.

He picked up the chair and sat, his eyes going straight to Skyler. "She looks so calm."

Cash nodded. "She's got an inner well of strength we could all only wish to have."

Cash was right. She was strong, and that strength came from God. Logan needed the same strength if he was going to keep his panic at bay and maintain a logical train of thought. He offered a heartfelt plea, hoping God would answer his prayers despite his absence in the past few years. Then Logan went to work.

"Maybe we can trace where the video is streaming from." He grabbed his phone and dialed Wagner to give him the web address.

"I'll get an analyst working on it," Wagner said. "But if Eaton's smart enough to pull off this abduction, he's likely bouncing the signal through proxy servers across the globe. I doubt we'll be able to find her this way."

Logan didn't want to hear it, but he knew Wagner was right. He looked at the video and another idea hit him.

"Hang on a minute, Wagner." Logan rewound the video to see if the taping started before the snow obscured the view. He started playing it again.

Cash tapped the screen. "Looks like something in the background."

Logan squinted. "A sign maybe, but I can't make out the words." He turned his attention to the phone. "I need this video enhanced."

"We can do that," Wagner said. "I'll have the tech download the file from the internet. If he can enhance the screenshot, I'll text it to you the second I have it."

Logan hung up and returned his focus to Skyler. Brave, strong Skyler. Only one word came to mind.

Home.

He'd come home. Not to Portland. Not to his family. But to Skyler. The woman who made his life more fulfilling. Real. Honest. Emotionally available Skyler.

He needed to do everything within his power to repair things between them for a chance at happiness he'd only have with her.

First, he needed to find her.

Jake stepped into the room. "Darcie called. Eaton didn't make it."

"Did he tell them where Skyler is?" Logan asked, then held his breath in fear of the answer.

Jake shook his head in slow, sorrowful arcs.

Logan slammed his fist on the desk.

"We'll find her," Jake said. "We all just need to stay calm and look for leads."

Panic rooting deep, Logan returned to browsing through the computer as the rest of the squad continued searching the house. His phone chimed. He grabbed it, nearly knocking it to the floor in his haste.

Can't trace the video. But here's a still shot of the sign.

"Thank you, Wagner." Logan thumbed to the enhanced photo. The sign was now quite readable.

"Perfect Peach Orchard," Cash mumbled. "Where in the world is that?"

A sunny day in October before Logan had left Skyler flashed into his mind. A day at the peach orchard filled with joy, laughter and love.

"I know exactly where it is." He glanced at the timer again. "We need to get out of here. It's a thirty-minute drive in good weather, and we don't have a second to waste."

In the truck, Darcie led the squad in prayer. As Jake drove, the rest of them made a plan. Not much of one if you asked Logan.

Cash would don his suit and go in alone while the others waited.

Logan didn't know if he could do that, but he'd try.

"I've got a live feed," Archer said, and the video of Skyler filled a monitor.

They all silently watched the video count down as the wind pummeled their truck.

Sixty minutes and thirty seconds.

Twenty-nine. Twenty-eight. Twenty-seven. Each second more precious than the last.

Cash, his expression tight, mumbled something under his breath, then started his arduous task of climbing into the heavy suit.

The computer lost its signal, the screen going black. Logan didn't know what was worse. Seeing the time counting down or not knowing if Skyler was okay. It was all he could do to stay seated. The minute Jake stopped the truck, he flew into the swirling snow.

He spotted the car, down a narrow path, a hundred feet in the distance. He took off, his feet slowed by the foot of snow blanketing the area.

Cash jerked him to a stop.

Logan spun on him and wrenched his arm free. "What are you doing, man? Skyler doesn't have much time. I need to get to her."

"You won't do her any good by running in there like a madman. Not only will you scare her, but there could be booby traps on the way that would blow us all to smithereens." Cash eyed him. "We're already taking a big risk not sending in the robot first, and I can't have you running rogue. Can you calm down enough to follow me or do I need to have Jake restrain you?"

Logan felt like a fool for letting his emotions get the best of him, but this was Skyler they were talking about here. His Skyler. The woman he loved.

"Well?" Cash asked pointedly.

Cash was right. Logan needed to calm down. He took a breath. "I can do it."

"Good. Stay behind me." Cash lifted his tools and swung his headlamp over the snow-covered ground. He moved forward at a snail's pace, nearly sending Logan over the edge of insanity.

He felt the timer counting down in his head, and his body vibrated with the need to race to Skyler. With ongoing pleas to God, Logan held himself in check. Barely. When they were within a few feet of the car, the world swam in front of his eyes, and he drew in a deep breath to keep the panic at bay.

They inched up to the driver's side.

"Skyler," Logan called softly to keep from startling her.

He heard her muffled plea from inside as Cash shone his headlamp on the door, then dropped to his knees and began carefully clearing snow from under the vehicle.

Logan knew Cash's precautions were necessary, but Logan needed to see Skyler and couldn't wait for Cash to finish. "Can I clear off the window?"

"Yes." Cash continued scooping out snow then set up his portable X-ray machine.

Logan swiped the window clean, the icy cold on his wrists clearing his emotions for the moment it took to look Skyler in the eye and telegraph his strength and conviction. Her eyes closed for a second, and then tears streamed down her face as she sobbed.

His heart ached for her. "I need to get her out of there."

"The door could be rigged. We can't risk opening it until I find the explosives, but we can make a hole in the window so you can remove the tape on her mouth." Cash struggled to his feet and cut a large circular opening.

After he removed the glass, Logan tossed his gloves to the ground and gently pulled the tape from Skyler's mouth while Cash went back to work.

"Logan," she croaked out as she looked up at him, relief burning in her eyes.

It was a good thing he was on the back side of the timer and couldn't see the remaining countdown or he might do something rash. He forced calm he didn't feel into his voice. "Hi, sweetheart."

"I didn't think anyone would find me. It was Tony Eaton's father."

"We know. We went to his house. There was a shoot-out. He didn't make it." At the pain sweeping into her eyes, Logan leaned closer to the hole and moved on. "Cash will defuse the bomb and we'll get you out of here, okay?"

"Yes, yes, please."

"Hey, squirt," Cash called out, his voice loaded with deep emotion so out of character for the big strapping guy.

"I'm so glad you're here, too!"

Logan looked Skyler over, spotted her raw and bloody wrists. Stifling a curse, he dug handcuff keys from his pocket. "Let's start by getting those cuffs off."

"Stay seated though, okay, squirt?" Cash added. "I don't know if there's a pressure sensor under your seat yet."

She nodded, and Logan set to work on gently removing the cuffs.

"Any idea where the explosives are?" Cash asked from the rear of the car where he'd moved the x-ray machine.

"Eaton mentioned the trunk and the wires he connected to the timer run in that direction." She winced as Logan took off the first cuff.

"Did you see explosives anywhere else?" Cash asked.

"None up front, but I didn't get a good look at the back-seat."

Logan withdrew the cuffs through the hole and her hands fell to her lap as if the muscles couldn't support them after hours in a raised position.

"I'll just snap a quick picture of the trunk then," Cash said. "I'd advise you to move back, Logan. For your own safety."

"No." Logan pocketed the cuffs and slipped his hand through the hole to rest it on Skyler's shoulder. She trembled, sending his anger burning to his core.

"Do what he says, Logan," she pleaded.

"No." He squeezed her shoulder. "I'm staying right here by your side. Don't even think of telling me to go."

"I don't want you to get hurt." Pleading eyes looked up at him.

"Cash will take care of us." He ached for more than a

simple touch of her shoulder. Ached to sweep her into his arms and never let go. And he wouldn't step back even for a moment.

Skyler let the warmth from Logan's hand, big and reassuring on her shoulder, seep into her body and help her relax. She heard Cash open the trunk and she glanced at the timer.

Ten minutes and counting down.

She had no idea if the bomb could be disabled. If anyone could do it, Cash could.

She didn't like Logan being in such danger, but she had to admit her heart was soaring at his presence. "I didn't expect you. I thought you'd be at the press conference."

"I'm sorry. So sorry. I hate the thought of you sitting here for hours thinking I wasn't coming for you." His forehead creased. If she could, she'd reach up and press the worry away.

"I screwed up again, Skyler. But it's the last time. I promise."

"Shh," she said. "It was my fault, too. I should've talked to you instead of slamming the door in your face." She smiled at him, hoping he could see her sincerity. "You must've missed the press conference. I'm sorry. You worked hard for the ASAC position."

"It doesn't matter anymore. I still want the job, but if Inman gives it to someone else—" he shrugged "—so be it. It took a while to get it into my pigheaded brain, but I finally realized you're more important than anything else."

He ran his hand over her hair, sending shivers trailing down her body.

"Family is more important than any job in the world," he continued. "So is love and that peace I saw on your face while I was watching the video. I was hyperventilating, ready to jump out of my skin, and death is staring you in the face, yet you were calm as can be."

"Trust me," she said, shaking her head. "I wasn't calm. At least not at first."

"But you found it, didn't you?" He smiled. "I admire your strength. Your faith and contentment. I can only hope you'll help me find them, too."

"What're you saying, Logan?" she asked, vaguely aware of Cash moving around the outside of the car, then climbing into the backseat, but she was too captivated by Logan to take her eyes from him.

"I want us to try again. We can do that, right?"

"Not with you in Chicago. If you didn't get the job, you'll have to go back there."

"I'm not going back to Chicago. At least not longer than it takes to resign and work out my notice."

"Resign? What will you do if you leave the FBI?"

"I'll find something else in Portland. As long as I'm with you, that's all that matters."

"We're clear." Cash joined them.

Skyler twisted to look at the timer, which had stopped at five minutes. Five minutes before all three of them would've been blown to bits. She shuddered and couldn't wait to leave the car. "Can I get out now?"

A rare smile lit Cash's face. "Yes. We're good."

Logan jerked the door open and knelt on the ground. She managed to swivel her body, stiff from the cold, and fall into his arms. He opened his mouth as if to speak, but then his lips came crashing down on hers instead. The intensity of his kiss proved his love, and she reveled in it. He was here for her. Now and forever.

Cash cleared his throat. "Um, guys? You're still on video."

Logan lifted his head and laughed. "Good! I want the

whole world to know that I'm in love with Deputy Skyler Brennan, and I want to spend my life proving that to her."

She wasn't used to such a public display of affection from him. "You love me?" she asked shyly.

He gazed into her eyes. "I do, Skyler. I love you."

"I love you, too." She twisted her head to look at the camera. "For the record, I love him, too."

He laughed before kissing her again and she knew the happiness she'd sought for so many years was finally hers.

"Look. We're top news." Skyler pointed at the TV in her condo.

Logan watched the bomb scare, all the way through his declaration of love, as it played on the screen. He squirmed in his seat, hating that his personal life was on TV for everyone to see. But he wasn't embarrassed that the world knew he loved the strong, amazing woman tucked under his arm.

"Is this too much?" he asked, not knowing how she felt about it. "Do you want me to turn it off?"

She looked up at him. "Are you kidding? Seeing you put me first and declare your love will never bother me." Her eyes warmed with love.

Unconditional love he'd strived his whole life to feel. His heart exploded with it, and he kissed her. Proving to himself that she really was there. That she was his. Now and forever.

He lifted his head and smiled at her.

"That will never bother me, either," she said in a teasing voice.

"Promise?"

"Hmm, maybe we should try it a few more times to be sure." She winked at him, and he kissed her again. Thoroughly. Completely.

When they broke apart, he heard the balding male anchor say, "This story of a man's and woman's courage and bravery in the face of losing it all has gone viral."

The female anchor nodded. "That's right. Social media has been flooded with comments about Agent Hunter's bravery. I have to admit to watching it over and over again myself. Seeing him stay with Deputy Brennan when he knew he could die…" She sighed.

Skyler smiled up at him. "With the way this is going, I'll have to fight women off you with a stick."

He caressed her cheek. "No need. I only have eyes for you."

"My turn to swoon." She laughed, then pointed at the screen, where the news team had transitioned to recorded video from the afternoon press conference. Though Inman mentioned Logan's role in heading up the robbery investigation, he didn't say a word about the promotion.

"Looks like I need to start looking for a job," Logan said. His cell rang from the coffee table, but he ignored it. He didn't want to talk with anyone other than Skyler.

She slipped out from under his arm and grabbed the phone. "It's Inman."

"Let it go to voice mail." Logan tried to pull her back.

"No." She handed it to him. "It could be about the job, and I want you to take it."

"Hunter," Logan answered and drew Skyler close so she could hear the call.

"You're getting quite a lot of publicity." Inman actually sounded impressed rather than mad. "Phones have been ringing off the hook at the office with people commending your bravery and dedication to Deputy Brennan."

"I didn't do it for the publicity or for the accolades."

"I didn't think you did, but we can't ignore the fact that in one night you've done more to eliminate any negative perception of the FBI than I've been able to accomplish in years."

"Grandstanding as usual," Logan mouthed for Skyler, and she shook her head.

"I'd be a fool to let you go back to Chicago and take the publicity with you. I was annoyed that you blew off the press conference, but you had a good excuse. So the ASAC job is still yours if you want it."

"Hmm," Logan said as if he might not take it. Skyler socked him in the arm.

"You do still want the job, don't you?" Inman asked.

"Yes," Logan replied. "But only if you accept the fact that I'll have a life outside the bureau. I'll give the job my all, but when it's time to go home—" he paused and locked eyes with Skyler "—I *will* be going home."

"I can work with that," Inman said. "We'll iron out the details in the morning."

Logan hung up and circled both arms around Skyler. "I have no idea how long he'll go along with my priorities, but I don't care. I've got a job in the same city as you, and that's all that matters."

He kissed her again, and the thought of their life together filled him utterly and completely with the peace he'd been seeking his entire life.

EPILOGUE

Twinkling white lights from the tree cast a warm glow over the family room, and the space rang with children's laughter. Shelter families milled around tables loaded with crafts, games and refreshments.

Perfection.

Just as Skyler had imagined since she'd put up the first strand of lights. But never had she imagined her heart would be overflowing with such joy. If Logan wasn't running late, her happiness would be uncontainable.

Is he coming?

The thought lingered for only the briefest of seconds before she put it out of her mind. She still needed to work on trusting that he'd be there for her as he promised, but with time she was certain she'd overcome her fears completely.

Movement in the snow-covered yard caught her attention, and her heart warmed even more. Archer, Brady, Jake and Cash, dressed in robes, played their roles in a live nativity scene. Though many of the shelter families weren't believers, she took this opportunity to share the real reason for Christmas along with providing the festivities they expected to see.

"Here Comes Santa Claus" suddenly pelted from speakers and Darcie entered the room dressed as Santa's elf, the jolly big man following her with "ho, ho, hos." She winked at Skyler, then escorted Santa to his impressive chair on the decorated platform by the fireplace.

Despite her joy, Skyler cringed for a moment. The same volunteer played Santa every year, and, though he had a good heart, he also had moments when he couldn't deal with distraught children and Skyler had to intervene.

No biggie. If that was her main problem tonight, it was minor.

She stepped closer to him and kept watch for any situation that Darcie couldn't handle, but everything went well. Swimmingly, in fact. Tonight Santa was amazingly warm and patient. Soon the line of children dancing with excitement as they waited dwindled down to four children. Still, as a three-year-old with curling pigtails and a trembling lower lip approached the platform, Darcie signaled for Skyler to come forward.

Skyler remembered the child's name was Zoe. She was a shy little thing, so Skyler knelt beside her. "Remember me, Zoe? My name's Skyler. We read together at the shelter."

Zoe nodded, her lip still trembling.

"Santa is my friend, and he's a very nice man," Skyler said. "Would you like me to take you to see him?"

She looked up at Santa then back at Skyler. "He's big."

"How about I sit on Santa's knee and hold you on my lap," she offered as she'd done for many children over the years.

Zoe nodded, and Skyler scooped her up. She smelled of baby shampoo and a soft little pigtail tickled Skyler's cheek as she passed Darcie to sit on Santa's knee. "Tell Santa what you want for Christmas, Zoe."

"Yes, sweetie, what do you want?" Santa said. The voice—though disguised—was one Skyler would recognize in her sleep.

She shot her head around to look into Logan's eyes, sparkling with impish humor and love for her. He slipped his arm around her waist, and she wished the room would empty for a moment so she could tug down his beard and kiss him in thanks for his kindness. Instead, the team, dressed in their Biblical garb, stepped inside, and Darcie squatted by the last three children in line, her eyes gleaming with satisfaction.

Something was up, but Skyler didn't know what. She'd just have to let things play out.

"I want a princess doll," Zoe said, now very serious and drawing Skyler's attention.

"Then Santa will see that you get one, honey," Logan said, making Skyler think about how wonderful he'd be with their children in the future, melting her heart into a big puddle.

Darcie climbed the platform and took Zoe from Skyler's arms. Skyler started to rise, but Logan stood and settled her on the chair. She looked out over the room. Her teammates lined the far wall. They watched with interest, and she suspected they were in on whatever was going to happen next.

Logan knelt in front of her and pulled a velvet box from under the bulky red coat. He opened it slowly, his eyes never leaving hers. "Skyler Brennan, will you do me the honor of becoming my wife? I promise I'll be there for you every day. Including all of the holidays. I'll do my best to make each and every one of them as special as you are."

Skyler's heart burst. It took a lot for the very prim and proper Logan to play Santa and let his emotions show for the children and for her in a public setting.

How could she resist such a man?

"Yes," she said. "I'll gladly marry you."

He slipped the ring on her finger. "In that case," he announced to the crowd, "Santa will be taking a quick break."

He scooped Skyler into his arms and stepped down from the platform. Darcie had cleared a path to the dining room, and he marched forward. Her teammates clapped Logan on the back as they passed. Their beaming smiles said they approved, adding even more happiness to this special day.

In the dining room, he set her down and ripped off his beard. "I was glad to do this tonight to surprise you, but promise me I won't have to play Santa every year."

"Of course you won't." She twined her arms around his neck and attempted a serious look. "We'll alternate. Some years you can be the Easter Bunny and others Cupid instead."

He threw back his head and laughed. She joined in until tears started streaming down her face.

He whisked them away with a thumb. "I'm hoping those are happy tears."

She nodded. "I love you, Logan."

"I love you, too." His expression sobered.

"What's wrong?"

"Promise me something."

"Anything."

"If I ever start to take you for granted and let work take over, promise you'll put me in my place so I can get my priorities right."

She grinned up at him. "I know it will never be necessary, but if it makes you feel better, I gladly promise."

He crushed her to him and kissed her, and she knew the battle they'd waged for so many years in search of love was over. A lifetime of happiness awaited them both.

* * * * *

Dear Reader,

I am so thrilled to bring you the first book in the First Responder series. I'm already fully immersed in the lives of the First Response Squad and hope you have enjoyed meeting the six-member team who race into danger at a moment's notice to protect the public from unexpected disasters. Each story in this series will revolve around finding peace in trying times, and I hope, as the team members search for peace in their own lives, that they will help you find more peace in yours.

If you'd like to learn more about this new series, stop by my website at www.susansleeman.com. I also love hearing from readers, so please contact me via email, susan@susansleeman.com, on my Facebook page, www.facebook.com/SusanSleemanBooks, or write to me at Love Inspired, 233 Broadway, Suite 1001, New York, NY 10279.

Susan Sleeman

Questions for Discussion

1. Logan lived his life through the lens of his father's high expectations. Have you ever had a parent or another role model in your life whose expectations were so high you didn't think you could meet them? If so, what did you do about it?

2. Logan let go of the pain his father caused, but we don't see in the story how he moves forward with his father. If you were Logan, what kind of relationship would you have with your father going forward?

3. Skyler's best friend, Darcie, tries to warn Skyler about Logan so she doesn't get hurt again. Have you ever warned a friend about to make what you saw as a big mistake? Did it help or did they resent you for your interference?

4. Logan is all about control. He thinks if he can control things, he will achieve his goals faster. Are you one who tries to control your life, or are you more like Skyler, approaching life from a laidback stance? Can you see how putting these two personalities together can make them stronger and yet cause friction?

5. Since this is the start of a new series, with each book featuring a member of the First Response Squad, which team member do you think you can most identify with now and why? I'll ask the same question in book six, and it will be fun to see if you still feel the same way.

6. Logan wanted his job promotion at any cost. Even the cost of losing his peace. Is there anything in your life

that you are letting rob you of your peace? A worry?
A desire? A hope? If so, can you give it to God and regain your peace?

7. This book takes place at Christmastime. A time when
we all think about peace. Do you know someone else
who is struggling to find peace in a difficult situation?
What one thing can you do today to help that person?

8. After Logan walked out on Skyler, she had to relearn
how to trust him. Have you ever had someone hurt
you so badly that you haven't been able to trust them
again? Does Skyler's story help you see how you might
work on that?

COMING NEXT MONTH FROM
Love Inspired® Suspense

Available December 2, 2014

HER CHRISTMAS GUARDIAN
Mission: Rescue • by Shirlee McCoy
Scout Cramer's young daughter is kidnapped while Scout is on the run from her troubled past. Can hostage rescue expert Boone Anderson risk his life—and his heart—to bring them together again?

THE YULETIDE RESCUE
Alaskan Search and Rescue • by Margaret Daley
A plane crash leaves Dr. Aubrey Mathison stranded in the Alaskan wilderness during the Christmas season. Search and Rescue leader David Stone arrives just in time, but together they'll discover there are more dangers lurking on the snowy horizon.

COLD CASE JUSTICE • by Sharon Dunn
Rochelle Miller thinks she's left her past behind as a witness to murder, until the criminal reappears. This time when she runs, she'll have handsome paramedic Matthew Stewart to keep her son safe...and the killer at bay.

NAVY SEAL NOEL
Men of Valor • by Liz Johnson
Abducted by a drug cartel, Jessalynn McCoy must rely on her former best friend—navy SEAL Will Gumble—to get her home in time for Christmas. But can she bring herself to trust the man who left her behind years ago?

SILVER LAKE SECRETS • by Alison Stone
After her life is put on the line, Nicole Braun refuses to allow her little boy to get caught up in the danger. Too bad the only one she can trust to protect her, police chief Brett Eggert, also has the power to break her heart.

TREACHEROUS INTENT • by Camy Tang
It's Liam O'Neill's job as a skip tracer to find private investigator Elisabeth Aday's missing client. When rival gangs come after them for information, they're thrown together in a race against the clock.

LISCNM1114

REQUEST YOUR FREE BOOKS!

2 FREE RIVETING INSPIRATIONAL NOVELS
PLUS 2 FREE MYSTERY GIFTS

Love Inspired®
SUSPENSE

YES! Please send me 2 FREE Love Inspired® Suspense novels and my 2 FREE mystery gifts (gifts are worth about $10). After receiving them, if I don't wish to receive any more books, I can return the shipping statement marked "cancel." If I don't cancel, I will receive 4 brand-new novels every month and be billed just $4.74 per book in the U.S. or $5.24 per book in Canada. That's a savings of at least 21% off the cover price. It's quite a bargain! Shipping and handling is just 50¢ per book in the U.S. and 75¢ per book in Canada.* I understand that accepting the 2 free books and gifts places me under no obligation to buy anything. I can always return a shipment and cancel at any time. Even if I never buy another book, the two free books and gifts are mine to keep forever.

123/323 IDN F5AC

Name	(PLEASE PRINT)	
Address		Apt. #
City	State/Prov.	Zip/Postal Code

Signature (if under 18, a parent or guardian must sign)

Mail to the Harlequin® Reader Service:
IN U.S.A.: P.O. Box 1867, Buffalo, NY 14240-1867
IN CANADA: P.O. Box 609, Fort Erie, Ontario L2A 5X3

**Are you a current subscriber to Love Inspired Suspense books
and want to receive the larger-print edition?
Call 1-800-873-8635 or visit www.ReaderService.com.**